Master of the Arts

Doug McPhillips

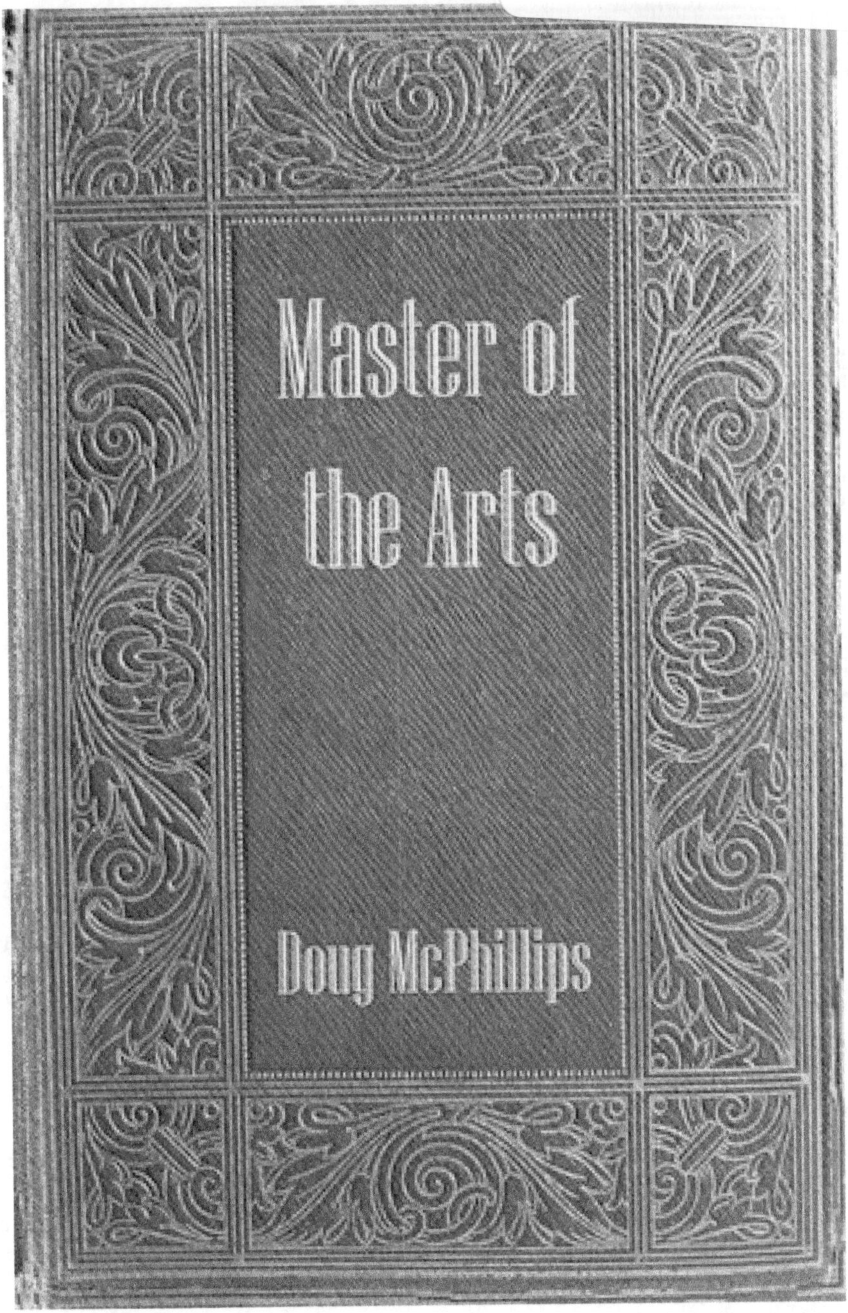

Also by Doug McPhillips:

Other Visionary Stories:
NOVELS.

From Darkness to Light
Awake to My Gutted Dream
The Sword of Discernment
Santiago Traveller
I'Prophet
Masters at my table
The Guru of Jerusalem
We Are Me Upside Down (Biography)
The Wicklow Way
The Adventures of Ace McDice,
Stretch Deed & Moonshine Melody
Instant Karma & Grace
The Credo
A Writer on the Rocks
Reincarnation of the Assassin
The One
Masters of Introspection:
A thesis on Suffering
The Rise and His of a Fourth Reich
A Camino Guide Book
Country Camino (Album)
Santiago Traveller (Album)
Soul Fact. (Album)

Doug McPhillips April 2023

ISBN. 978-0-6486214-6.

National Library of Australia Catalogue- in -publication data:
Stories of Roland Told to Children. H.G.Marshall Barnes and Noble 2023
Stories of Roland James Baldwin Barnes and Noble 2006
The Travels of Marco Polo, "The Milione," Rustichello da Pisa, 13th Century.
The Merchant of Venice. William Shakespeare was published in 1598.
Google research-Authors Unknown.

Introduction

Rustichello da Pisa is the main character of this story. The author has given him the title of Master of the Arts. He was a philosopher, romance and travel writer but apart from his talents recorded in the historical records he was never a Master of Arts as depicted in this story. It is for this frictional account that he has acquired the title and much of what is attributed to him in myth is recorded here in *italics*

This is a blended genre story of the facts and fictitious events surrounding the lives of Marco Polo and Rustichello da Pisa. Marco spent 17 years in the court of Kublai Khan, gaining favour with the Khan and eventually becoming one of his trusted diplomats. After Marco returned to Venice employed in the family merchant business, he got involved in the city's war with Genoa and was imprisoned with trusted friend and confidant Rustichello da Pisa. It was during their imprisonment that Marco told his story to Rustichello about his service to The Khan of Khans in Asia and his many adventures beyond the confines of the known world. Rustichello journaled a manuscript entitled "The Travels of Marco Polo." Whilst this story was read far and wide throughout Europe at the time it was nonetheless eclipsed by the stories and talents of the author's life himself, for Da Pisa's adventures gained him much notoriety in later life as " A Master of The Arts."

Marco Polo (1254-1324) was a Venetian merchant believed to have journeyed across Asia at the height of the Mongol Empire. He first set out at
age 17 with his father and uncle, travelling overland along what later became known as the Silk Road. Upon reaching China, Marco Polo entered
the court of powerful Mongol ruler Kublai Khan, who dispatched him on
trips to help administer the realm. Marco Polo remained abroad for 24
years. Though not the first European to explore China—his father and uncle, among others, had already been there—he became famous for his travels thanks to a popular book he co-authored while languishing in a Genoese
prison where he met the Arthurian adventure writer Rustichello of Pisa,
with whom he would collaborate on a 1298 manuscript called "Description
of the World." Later to be known as "The Travels of Marco Polo." With the
help of notes taken during his adventures, Marco Polo reverently described
Kublai Khan and his palaces, along with paper money, coal, postal service,
eyeglasses and other innovations that had not yet appeared in Europe. He
also told partially erroneous self-promoting tales about warfare, commerce,
geography, court intrigues and sexual practice. Marco Polo returned home
after a Genoese-Venetian peace treaty in 1299. He married and had three
daughters. He continued to trade in his golden years. Marco died in January
1324. Everything we know about him comes from his text. Asian sources
never mentioned him. He was a raconteur but like da Pisa could not be clas-
sified as a Master of Arts.

This story is a tale of tragedy, loss of material wealth, courage and determination to succeed in the face of great odds. It's a tale of adventure, change in direction and philosophy of life which carried Rustichello into many fields of endeavour as it had done for his friend Marco Polo. It is fitting that this tale be told of men of many talents and how they utilised their God-given gifts ultimately in the service of others. If the facts and fiction of the tale had not been told it would be just a whiff of smoke in the scheme of things and a pity beyond the imagining.

This tale tells extensively of the life of Rustichello's entry into the halls of Philip III, King of France (1270–85) services, in whose reign the power of the monarchy was enlarged and the royal domain extended, though his foreign policy and military ventures. It is a delightful lesson in the importance of perseverance for him as to any man to find his rightful place in the world, for it was the slings and arrows of outrageous fortune that he was called upon initially to adapt his chameleon talents to the outer world as well as holding in reserve his inner divine commitment. De Pisa proved flexible and discerning in his ability; a juxtaposition of masking his part divinity and at the same time his ability to be a trickster, to gain favour with the King, to reflect his various talents to gain a position of importance for his immediate survival in service. Although the immediate vocation in the King's service necessitated money it was not a recognised profession in the accrual of monitory needs that was da Pisa's deep-down motivation. He would find in time, despite his many God-given talents that his real purpose involved his heart's desire for him to ultimately find his place in life as a philosopher, travel writer and writer of romance novels.

The scene opens as the curtain is drawn back on the court of King Phillip 111 as a great assembly of the people meets. He had a personal invitation to those present to enjoy a feast and entertainment to celebrate the King's appointment to the throne. And so the stage is set for Rustichello to enter the great assembly and convince the newly appointed King of France, Phillip 111, of his talents and in the telling to relate his connection with the young Marco Polo whilst in the services as a Merchant in Venice in the employment of Marco's father Niccolò and his uncle Maffeo. It is in the proof of his talents and the telling of his story that the king is impressed with the young man's abilities and the courage he portrays to overcome misfortune in the face of much adversity. We shall tell first of duty in his service to the King of France as a Master of the Arts and later of his adventurers.

'Master of the Arts' may be too vast a collection of talents for any human to aspire to, and usually, such mastery is not required when we apply for a job. But this story tells of Rustichello de Pisa which tells us that we may need to acquire a variety of skills if we are to find a place in our constantly changing world. This medieval tale is strangely parallel to this author's life, as it may be yours, in that it is up-to-date because it presents us with the importance of acquiring knowledge of many related subjects even if we aspire to work at only one. The idea of specialising and becoming good at just one thing may have been appropriate decades ago; the job market and the creative arts then were different, as the computer age had not begun and AI was not the benefit nor threat as it now is.

Now the world is changing with incredible rapidity, and we need to acquire the mercurial all-roundness of a Rustichello if we are to beat the competition and make our way towards our world goals. Equally, we must balance the heart in tune with the mind to become one who lives in this world but at the same time is not of it. That is to say have the faith, the courage of one's convictions, to use our God-given talents in as much as to provide for ourselves as to be of service to others.

It is to be noted that Rustichello, throughout this story, was always persistent in his endeavours, and equally in this quality it is proven that it is vital if in life we are to make our aspirations real. Rustichello does not go away in a depressed start when rejection comes his way, nor does he get angry or arrogant; he simply counters the refusal with another offer. He knows that he does not need to be the best at any job. His natural talent is worthy of being capable before several other people in terms of the resourcefulness he has to offer because he believes in himself, a self-aggrandising vision, based on practical experience. He is a man who is capable of doing the job of six men. Rustichello is a thoroughly modern person and is well aware of market forces. There are deep and meaningly profound issues concerning the way of life this man of vision lived which we explore through this mythical tale, but let us now begin with getting our feet planted firmly on the ground. "

Comment by the author.

CHAPTER 1

KEYS TO THE KINGDOM

Ten years after he became heir to the throne on the death of his elder brother Louis (1260) and after accompanying his father's crusade against Tunis in 1270, he was in Africa when King Louis IX died, the younger son Phillip 111 of France was anointed King at Reims. So on this day in 1271, the King held a great assembly at the Royal Palace of Paris to celebrate his coronation, to which he invited nobles, politicians, kings of far-off provinces and a selection of the peoples of the Catholic faith to a grand feast in his honour in the Royal assembly hall. Whilst the feast was at its height and those present were being entertained by those appointed to do so by the King, a stranger, clothed like a king himself, came to the palace gates. The Gardes du Corps du Roi (king's bodyguards) signalled the porter in charge of entry to the great hall of assembly who asked him his name and errand.

" I am Rustichello da Pisa," the stranger replied: " I am a merchant of Venice, a knight of the Templar order, and the grandson of Italian nobility of Pisa. " he responded.

"Oui, Oui," the porter said impatiently, then reverted to the English parlé to annoy the stranger. "but I did not ask you for your genealogy. What is your profession? For no one is admitted here unless he is a master of some craft."

"Well as I already said I am a merchant from Venice, but as to profession you may announce me to the king as a Master of the Arts." Rustichello pauses, and before the Porter could respond, he says: " I seek an audience with the King as he needs my services." The porter was a little puzzled by this response but could see by the presence of the man that he would not take no for an answer from a king's porter, so with part-tongue-in cheek replied: "Wait a while here and I will see if the King will give you an audience." As the Porter turned to walk away Rustichello called out; " Ask the King if he has with him a man who is master of all crafts at once, for if he has then I do not need an audience with him."

So the porter went inside and told the king that a man had come who called himself Rustichello of Lugh Ioldanach, which means " The Master of all Arts", and that he claimed to know everything. So the King requested his best swordsman to go out and challenge the stranger to a sword fight to test the man's physical dexterity and he also sent his best chess player to challenge the man's mental ability and resolve. It seems in no time at all that the Porter was again by the side of the King to report that 'Rustichello had quickly disarmed the King's swordsman and in three straight moves had defeated the chess master.' The King could see that his porter was duly impressed by the stranger and eagerly announced the stranger's swordsmanship and chess ability was " Rustichello's enclosure" which is what he had told the porter to tell the King. So he was invited in and Rustichello without a prompt from the King sat himself down upon the chair called the 'sage's seat,' which was kept for the wisest man.

The King overlooked the impropriety of Rustichello in taking up without asking for a place of importance in the assembly. " So what is it that you want from me? He inquired.

" I am seeking a position in your kingdom, perhaps as a carpenter for I am quite skilled with my hands in that craft."

"May I enquire how you obtained that skill?" the King enquired. Rustichello replied; " I worked for a time as a carpenter's assistant building Mary, the Holy Virgin ship for the merchant's fleet and in designing and building storehouses for the Polo brothers, merchants in Venice. "

The King paused for a while head in hand watching the strong man entertain. As if in passing he replies to Rustichello "We already have several boat builders, skilled carpenters and masters apprentices, I am in no need of another."

Patiently Rustichello, looking a the strength of the strong man bending a steel bar for the king's pleasure, states: " I am skilled as a blacksmith too."

The King replies, "We already have one of those, we don't need another." Rustichello suggested another of his capabilities.

" I was a leader of a Knights Templar troop for several years and I'm a professional warrior."

" We do not need one. Our strongman here Omega is our champion who also was a knight before I employed him."

Rustichello notices that the King is relaxing no doubt having the savage beast lulled by the steady play of his harpist."" I too am a harpist." says Rustichello, " but I also can make up lyrics for the king's pleasure and melodies that will calm the mind."

The King responded: "I have a harpist, a poet laureate and several musicians who can make up melodies that inspire me. I am in no need of another."

The King watches as the strongman lifts a large boulder above his head and attempts to throw it like a shot put across the assembly room. "I am more than just a strong man, for I am renowned as a warrior of great skilfulness rather than mere strength," says Rustichello. The King responds " I am content with whom I have."

"I am a great storyteller and writer of many romantic tales," says Rustichello." Then the King a little impatient now says "As I have already indicated to you, I have poets, storytellers and writers of renown. I am in no need of such services."

Rustichello now realising that action speaks louder than words was seeking to demonstrate some of his abilities. He watched the King's champion Omega showing off his strength by pushing a flagstone so large that it had taken four oxen to move it there. The stone was only a portion of a much larger rock nearby. Rustichello made his way across the assembly floor and with one hand lifted the smaller stone and placed it on top of the larger stone. Then he picked up the harp and began to sing a melody of his composition that lulled the king and his guests into a temporary slumber before he began to play a sad composition that made all those present weep. To finish his little bracket of songs he sang a jolly old reel that he played by ear and all the assembly laughed with joy.

It was then that the king saw the numerous talents of this stranger and realised that one so gifted could be of great help to his people against his enemies. So he dismissed the assembly after the feasting and took counsel with his chief advisers of the Realm, advising Rustichello to come to the throne room in one hour after he returned from his afternoon nap. Of course, the king did not need sleep but instead devised a plan for the appointed time of his calling Rustichello to the throne room. The counsel with theorists of his court had advised him to lend the throne to Rustichello in six weeks hence whilst the King took time out to visit the far-off provinces of his kingdom. He intended to make Rustichello his war leader for the whole of the kingdom as there was much unrest in areas of the province due to the influence of the Moors holding territories formerly ruled by the Catholic Church and ultimately by the King of France himself. The King wished to take charge of his larger kingdom and sought to remove the Moor armies from the kingdom and distant holdings. So he could see in this man of numerous talents that he needed this warrior of extraordinary ability. But King Philip knew to test this stranger first before he handed over the kingdom to him temporarily for the time of his absence. He had a wish to visit far-off places to devise a plan to rid the kingdom of the Mongol menace.

King Philip summoned Rustichello before him and enquired as to his need for service. " And how is it that a merchant of Venice who would supposedly be rich in material possessions would need to be in service to my kingdom?" He paused then continued.: "Tell me what happened to inspire you to darken my door?" Rustichello then began to explain what tragedy had befallen him and to prove his need for employment at the bidding of his king.

Rustichello began: "It was in 1260 that I finished building a storehouse for the travelling merchants Nicollo and Maffelo Polo. The brothers had been in business for many years before I began working for them, for they had established trading posts in Constantinople, Sudan in Crimea, and a western part of the Mongol Empire in Asia. As a duo, they reached modern-day China before temporarily returning to Europe to deliver a message to the Pope from the then King of Mongolia. At the time of their first journey to China, Niccolo left his young son behind in the care of his cousin's family as his wife had died. They were to supervise his education through the Catholic system learning the length and breadth of Latin and Greek. I was assigned to help teach the growing lad the ways of buying and selling merchandise mainly supplied from Portugal in Porto. I was given charge over all of Europe for buying and exporting purchases from their trade centre in Venice. At this time, the two brothers had been living in the Venetian quarter of Constantinople where they resided for several years."

"It was there they enjoyed diplomatic immunity, political chances and tax relief because of Italy's role in establishing the Latin Empire However, I got word from a ship's captain that they were unwinding their merchant business and transferring northeast to Sudak, a city in the Crimea, as the city of Constantinople had become politically precarious as you would no doubt be aware my King, for you to had been in service there for a time with your father during the war that followed. "

"When I received word again from a ship's captain that Constantinople was recaptured by the then ruler of the Empire of Nicaea who had promptly burned and razed the Venetian quarter to the ground, capturing all Venetian citizens who were then blinded and those who did escape aboard overloaded refugee vessels bound for Venetian colonies died at sea. I was relieved to know my employers were safe in their new location and I would have to grow the business in Europe at best awaiting their return."

"So it was I who travelled to Lisbon, Porto and other places along the Portuguese coastline; ports of call for the purchase of honey, animal hides, olive oil, figs and other commodities that I shipped from Portugal at Porto and transported also via the Port of Venice destined for England at some of the English King's colonies. It was on such a trip earlier this year that tragedy befell me. Before leaving Venice I had no one other than my wife to handle finances in my absence. I had arranged with a Jewish money lender a line of credit to fund the journey and ample monies to cover the purchase of commodities to purchase and trade on behalf of my employer in my absence. I had given my wife power of attorney over all worldly possessions and the authority to call on the Jewish moneylender to borrow money when in need. I mistakenly entrusted my love with an open line of credit to borrow as she willed without imposing any restrictions. The Jewish bankers held as security in this instance a hold over all my possessions including a family villa, a boat and a stable for my horses of which I had paid in advance a stable hand to feed and exercise until my return."

Rustichello paused for a moment to catch his breath and requested a drink to clear his throat. The king ordered a servant to pour him a glass of wine, as he could see his intended charge was showing signs of distress. Rustichello, having drunk the wine, composed himself very quickly for he was not given to personal emotions and continued:

" I was absent from Venice on my Master's behalf in Portugal for three months before returning to Venice with a large quantity of supplies preordered and bound for England. In the meantime, my dear wife had taken a lover, squandered much of our wealth and using the line of credit to the full left with her lover and my dearly beloved children to places unknown, leaving me with an empty house, and a debt to the Jewish moneylender who began hounding me for his pound of flesh."

"After paying myself enough money to survive from the profit of those commodities destined for England, and giving what remained as an act of faith and goodwill to the Jewish moneylender who had a hold over my all, I got his agreement that he would not sell all that I once possessed until I could pay him back, giving me three months from that date to clear the debt or he would sell all that I had accumulated. So having an empty warehouse owned by my employer and no visible means of support I have traveled here with the little that now remains. For I sold my horse on the outskirts of Paris to hire a coach to arrive at your house of assembly in the style to which I was formally accustomed and I stand before you in the best of what I have left of clothing for my arrival here today to earn your trust and employment."

The King then related his need to travel to relieve his concerns about the dangers of the Moors holding territories on the outskirts of his southern borders and in the North in the hands of the rebellious bandits of the Spanish Pyrenees mountains. He was also destined on behalf of the Pope to drive the Moors out of Spain, in particular in the Iberian Peninsula. So he intended to leave Rustichello in charge, but with three provisions before this could take place " You have but six weeks to complete three tasks on my behalf before my ultimate decision to appoint you as a warrior leader and leave you for a time in charge of my kingdom.."

"Firstly, I want you to walk the Camino de Santiago from St. Jean Pied de Port at the base of the Pyrenees mountains to Santiago de Compostela in the far north of Spain on the Iberian peninsula. I want you to carry a burden representing my sin in the form of a bag of gold nuggets to lay at the altar in the Cathedral at the place where the ashes of St James reportedly lay."

Then the King with his hand on his chin in a contemplation way continued: "I will give you another small bag of gold to cover the cost of your journey. In addition, you may take from the sack of gold nuggets and give a nugget to any beggar along The Way and stave off your Jewish banker for a time by sending him some of the gold from my bag and whoever you consider is of a greater need for help than the sin I carry in my heart." King Philip never disclosed what that sin was nor did Rustichello think it any of his business other than to carry the burden of gold upon his own back for the sake of the King's relief of sin, the bag of gold, the majority of which was destined for the Santiago de Compostela Cathedral.

King Philip continues: "You have two other tasks to complete in the allotted time of six weeks before you return here. Firstly under the cloak of being a pilgrim continue your journey to the cape at Finisterre and roam the wild coastline in this isolated part going first to the village of Muxía. This path is less travelled than the fishing village of Finisterre, and whilst it has a sense of the wild sea and is the idyllic countryside for the heart of a poet such as yourself, you will remain as vigilant as a female servant in casting your net wide to see what stronghold the Moors have in the area. Then on your way back to Finisterre count the number of troops you encounter in your travels. Remember you will appear as a pilgrim on the route and if asked you will answer 'that you wish to cast your sin into the sea' in the form of the shirt that you wear and pray at the little stone church built by St. James at Muxía in devotion to the Virgin Mary at the cliff face."

"And what is the third task, my King?" Rustichello enquires. "It is to return to me via the Camino lower route from Roncesvalles. For it is there I want you to extract from a rock the Sword of Roland that has been embedded there since the time of the great General Charlemagne upon his retreat from Spain after wars with the Moors in the 700s ventures. You as a poet would no doubt know of Roncesvalles and

Valcarlos where the battle of Roland took place. It has been immortalised in the 'Song of Roland.' It is the earliest of our French epic poetry from centuries ago." Rustichello, not being a buff of French poetry had to admit that he was not aware of the Roland Song, but knew of the great battles of General Charlemagne. So King Philip 111, the newly crowned King of the Realm of the Kingdom of France took the the opportunity to enlighten him:

Then King once again reminded Rustichello of the three assigned tasks he would have to complete for him that he would then relinquish his throne for three months after which he would appoint him the leader of all his knights and military troops throughout the land. In addition, he would provide Rustichello with a purse to clear his debt to the Jewish money lender, to regain his earthly possessions, villa, horses and stables, and provide him with enough money to trade again on behalf of the Polo brothers before they returned to Venice from their travels.

Of course, the King being a man of cunning plots had not intended to release Rustichello from his duties to him that easily. He believed the young man had no chance of completing the third task of extracting the Sword of Roland from its embedded place in the rock. According to the Song of Roland, the legendary sword called 'Durandal' was first given to Charlemagne by an angel. It contained one tooth of Saint Peter, the blood of Saint Basil, the hair of Saint-Denis, and a piece of the raiment of the Blessed Virgin Mary, and was supposedly the sharpest sword in all existence. Roland as the story goes had relinquished the sword when the soldiers under his command fell to the Moor enemy and he was overpowered by the giant whom he had fought for days before being defeated by him. When he fell, before his dying breath, he had reportedly embedded the sword in a gap in the boulder rock nearby intent on snapping it in two so that it did not fall into the hands of the enemy. At his death, like his manifested belief in Jesus, the sun darkened and the earth trembled, an earthquake briefly erupted moving the rocks closer together, thus rendering the sword an impossible task to remove and it was now lying on its side within the rock face as Roland took his last breath.

So the King intended to honour all bar the release of his charge, to keep the Master of Arts as a warrior in his service until the time that the Moors could be driven from the lands. Once the lands were back in the realm of the Kingdom of France he would honour the third promise to release Rustichello from his duty to him. The King felt he had his intentions for his charge in the bag, as it were, for he believed that it was a virtual impossibility to remove Durandel, the sword of Roland, from the rock in which it was embedded. Many a strongman, soldier, king and Knight of the Templar had attempted over the centuries to remove it from its hold. Some had used various oils to try to loosen it, others had attempted to chisel it out and still, others had added rope and pull to attempt to extract it from its place of rest, but none had been successful in removing the sword from the stone. The King himself had once visited the sight of the Durandal sword and attempted to remove it but to no avail. He had felt that in his cunning in eliciting the agreement of Rustichello to complete all three tasks he had the upper hand on his charge. To entrap him in not allowing his release from duty to him so easily.

So Philip 111 king of France, in his proposal to Rustichello, sought to provide his charge with a history lesson of St James preaching the gospel of Christ's message and that it was by action and not words alone if one is to live a divine life. It is thus reinforced by the importance of Camino's journey in his mission to be forgiven his sin. In addition, he asked that Rustichello keep a daily journal of his experiences and prayers that he utter forgiveness of the sin of the King to no one on the Camino Way. He also particularly requested that he assist other pilgrims struggling on their pilgrimage in the King's name.

The King had his scribe write down all that he told Rustichello, for he believed that it was essential his mission be carried out to the letter. The King was also anxious to know of any strange rituals, witchcraft or mythical practices that influenced the inhabitants of his people on this Camino route. He wanted to know the mindset of those Rustichello met from Spain, their belief in a greater God, and if offerings were being made to the Catholic Church of which he belonged at the chapels on the route. Equally, the King requested all be journalised in a book for his future reference. He then dictated that no information of a military nature on the presence of Moor soldiers be recorded. He needed such matters of importance to be committed to memory for later recall and the King's ears only. It was then the King referred to his need for Rustichello to recover the sword of Roland and he thus began to point out its significance. He then explained his great desire for Durandal, the sword of Roland, and its significance for the kingdom in his future securing of the kingdom, against his enemies. He provided Rustichello, firstly with a journal for recording his pilgrimage and then a quill and ink with which to write down his daily experiences of The Way.

Rustichello was sent by the King to his archivist room to read the documents there on the great General Charlemagne and the story of Roland, for he wanted his charge to understand his mission, the road that he must travel, the mountainous route from St. Jean Pied de Port to Santiago, being The Way of St. James. It was St. James who preached the message of Christ's suffering and sacrifice, and that it was one thing to believe but that 'action speaks louder than words.' It was there that he read how Charlemagne, also known as Charles the Great or Charles I, was the King of France from 768 and the King of Italy from 774, and by 800 was the first emperor in Western Europe since the collapse of the Western Roman Empire three centuries earlier. The documents detailed the expanded French state, and how he founded the Carolingian Empire. It was Charlemagne who was considered to be the greatest ruler of the Carolingian Dynasty because of the achievements he made during what seemed like the very middle of the Dark Ages. To do this he launched a thirty-year military campaign from 772 to 804 of conquests that united Europe and spread Christianity. Charlemagne was engaged in almost constant battle throughout his reign, often at the head of his elite bodyguard squadrons, with his legendary sword "Joyeuse "in hand.

Rustichello read the accounts of his 46-year reign during which Charlemagne enjoyed unparalleled military victories, conquering most of Western Europe. From the Atlantic coasts of France to the west, the northern half of Italy to the south, modern-day Austria and Germany to the east, and north up to the North Sea, Charlemagne ruled it all. He never lost in battle but once, and it was under the leadership of his nephew Roland that the defeat transpired, for the young brave warrior and Charlemagne's rear guard of war-weary soldiers were slaughtered when caught by surprise by a band of Basque bandits and Muslims when retreating through the narrow pass on the lower route of the Camino, on the way back to France from the war against the Moors on that fate filled day August 15,778. Unlike Charlemagne's other hearty battles that he won, it was the defeat of Roland that was recorded into infamy. So before Rustichello continued reading Roland's famous battle to the death, he summoned the court lute player to sing for him the immortalised La Chanson de Roland The Song of Roland, the epic poem to get himself in a melancholy disposition to feel the sense of Roland's finale.

CHAPTER 2.

THE STORY OF ROLAND

Rustichello listened with intent to the poetic singing of the King's musician of the epic tale written some 100 years before for the benefit of the King and his court, The *Chanson de Roland* based on the Battle of Roncevaux may well have been mythical to some degree thought Rustichello, but in this poem, Roland is poetically associated with his unbreakable sword Durendal, various Christian relics, his horse Veillantif, and his Oliphant horn. This is what held the most interest to Rustichello, Master of Arts, for he knew that he needed to take all the facts and the myths of the story into account if he had any hope of recovering the sword for his king as his final task in carrying out his duty. For in his death stance, the Master of the Arts knew that Roland's disposal of the famous sword Durendal was still a fact. It was still embedded in a rock on the lower Camino Way between Ronces-valles and Valcarlos villages in that narrow gorge where the famous battle had taken place 12 centuries beforehand. At least that is how history had recorded it and the song of Roland had mythologised it.

Like Leonardo da Vinci and Michelangelo had done in dissecting human bodies to explore the body's inner workings so that they could display more accurately the human form in their sculptures and paintings from the inside, as Rustichello did with the story of Roland. For it was in the years that fol-lowed his death that Roland became an iconic figure and his heroic death at Roncevaux Pass was given mythical dimensions in medieval and later in Renaissance literature. But for the moment Rustichello was hearing the Song of Roland and reading the first and most famous of these heroic tales of the battle of Roncevaux Pass. It reported Basque mountain warriors with two short swords who made surprise attacks from the rocky cliffs of the narrow pass and with bows and javelins from a distance used as missile weapons killed many of the remainder of Charlemagne's rear guard.

Rustichello was reading an old scroll that related to when almost all of Roland's men were dead and he was left standing alone, badly injured and near death, he attempted to break his sword to prevent it from being taken by the Moors. For the last time, he blew his Olifant (his carved ivory hunt-ing horn created from elephant tusks). Roland had blown his Olifant horn with all his might and burst his temples and eardrums in the effort. The ef-fect of the sound of the horn was heard in the distant Pyrenees hills by

Charlemagne and his troops. Even though he knew that Charlemagne's army could no longer save them, he wanted to prevent the desecration of the bodies of the French soldiers in his rear guard. When he sensed that death was very near, he tried with all his might to break his great sword in between two large boulders to render it useless to his enemies. That is when the earth moved in a quake and trapped his precious Durandal deep within rocks. Then he laid himself down with his head on the grass, putting his horn under him, and turned his face toward his foe. When Charlemagne and his men reached the battlefield they found the bodies of Roland and his men. Legends say that Roland was laid to rest in the Basilica at Blaye, near Bordeaux.

The document Rustichello da Pisa, the Master of Arts, was reading recorded that on the night of August 15, 778, a large group of Basque guerrilla warriors ambushed the French rearguard. Charlemagne and the rest of the army were further ahead across the mountains, but an estimated 2,000 men in the rearguard were outnumbered and overwhelmed by the Basque forces. Roland and the rearguard held the Basques off long enough to allow Charlemagne and the rest of the Frankish army to get across the mountains unharmed. Charlemagne and his army had been returning from six years of battling Muslim Spain. He had entrusted his favoured and most beloved nephew in charge of his rear guard warriors, but his brother and stepfather, Ganglion, was left in charge of relaying a message back to the Muslim King in Pamplona, some seventy kilometres on the plain to the north beyond the Pyrenees, that Charlemagne was almost back on French soil, that he would accept the bribe of a bag of gold nuggets offered by the King to cease the war and was leaving in peace. Ganglion who was now under Roland's command, had quarrelled with him before leaving for his appointed task because Ganglion was jealous of Roland's position with Charlemagne. Ganglion went to the Muslim leader and revealed Charlemagne's route back to France, suggesting that in the narrow pass through the Pyrenees, the rear guard would be more vulnerable and once defeated the majority of the French army could then be defeated by a surprise attack from the rear. He pocketed the gold destined for Charlemagne and waited far back and out of the trap that awaited Roland and the troops in the Roncesvalles Pass. The Muslim king felt justified in hiring a group of Basque assassins in his service, for the Basque attack was in retaliation for Charlemagne's destruction of the city walls of their capital, Pamplona.

Charlemagne had heard the sound of his nephew Roland's Olifant (Elephant) horn, for Roland had left it until there was no more hope before he called for help. He intended to keep Charlemagne and the majority of the retreating but triumphant troops out of harm's way of the Barque forces that with the assistance of the Muslim's kings army had far outnumbered the rearguard troops, but Roland's final horn blast warning had alerted Charlemagne and allowed him the opportunity to attack head-on the Basque forces with the majority of his troops giving chase. Charlemagne returned to the call of Roland to find a bloodstained valley with all of his rear guard and his beloved nephew dead. In great grief he decided to turn his troops homeward and not launch another attack on the Moors, for under the sad circumstance of the death of Roland and his rear guard he had enough of war for the time being.

Ganglion justified his being both a spy for the Basque warriors, the Moors King in Pamplona and a traitor to Charlemagne and Roland concluding that "his madness will surely bring him to ruin" for he considers "the madness of arrogance, of loving war and its glory too much for a leader of a limited experience." However, the fact alone that Roland was able to rally his rear guard troops and strike fear in his enemy in battle by his bravery despite being outnumbered and trapped in a narrow pass where his Barsque bandits had the upper hand and knew the area better he could have easily retreated. Despite all this, he instead decided to fight the enemy alone without asking for reinforcement from Charlemagne who was marching ahead. Roland's vigour, strength, selflessness, pride, and faith are depicted characteristically in his reply to Olivier his friend and number two in command, who urged him to blow his horn and call Charlemagne for help: Roland's reported response was " A man should suffer greatly for his lord, endure both biting cold and sweltering heat and sacrifice for him both flesh and blood."Even though the French troops fought bravely and endured the terrifying onslaught, doing whatever was humanly possible, they continued to fight, even though they were outnumbered and condemned to perish one after another. They all fought courageously that day, but no one showed the kind of bravery Roland did. He pierced a multitude of enemies with his mighty spear and when the spear trembled in his hand, he took his unbreakable sword, Durandal, and smote man after man to the ground until he was overcome.

Rustichello da Pisa was anxiously searching the archival records for more information on Roland and what had become of the Ganglion after he had betrayed Charlemagne and helped set the trap for the demise of Roland and the rear guard troops. Not content with the limitation of the story of the song of Roland, he began to dig a little deeper into Roland's life as a younger man. He soon found written evidence of Roland's first battle on the side of his uncle Charlemagne in the early stages of the seven-year war against the Moors. And in his bloody battles to further the cause of the Pope in forcing pagans to turn to Christianity. It is then that Rustichello reads of Charlemagne's gift of the singing sword, Durandal, to Roland. He was only sixteen at the time when he went to his first battle.

It was recorded that Roland was a fearsome warrior of might and strength. In killing his enemy he swung the sword wildly over his head in the on-slaught of his enemy and it seemed to ring a sacred note which was attributed to the fact that it had the relics of the saints and the Virgin Mary embedded in its handle. Upon investigation, Rustichello discovered that Durandal was one of the four Holy Swords forged through the means of alchemy and magic. It was written that they were all on par having been forged similarly. Durandal is said to have mysterious origins, either brought to the West by the Moors of the East or created by Wayland the Smith, the mythical creator of other mythic swords including, Charlemagne's Joyeuse.

Seven years before, when Charlemagne had first come to Spain, King Marsil had sent a message to the old Emir of Babylon, begging him for aid. But Babylon is far, and the Emir Baligant had to gather his knights and barons from forty kingdoms, so the years passed and no help came. But now at last, after a long delay, he had reached the land of Spain and was even now sailing up the Ebro with all his mighty men of war. By day the river for miles was bright with gilded ship bows and many-coloured swallowtail flags By night thousands of lanterns glittered from the masts and swung and flickered in the summer breeze so that the country all around was lighted up with starry flame.

At length, the Emir landed. A white silk carpet was thrown upon the ground, in the shade of a laurel tree an ivory chair was set and there the Emir took his seat. Around him stood seventeen kings together with knights and barons in such numbers that no man might count them.

'Listen, valiant warriors,' cried Baligant. 'I mean to bring this Charlemagne, of whom we hear such wondrous tales, so low that he shall not even dare to eat unless I give him leave. Too long hath he been making war in Spain, and I will carry battle and the sword into his fair France. I shall never cease from warring until I see him at my feet, or dead.' And thus insolently boasting, Baligant struck his knee with his glove.

Then the Emir called two of his knights. 'Go to Saragossa,' he said, 'and tell King Marsil that I have come to help him. And what battle there will be when I meet Charlemagne! Give Marsil this glove embroidered with gold; put it on his right hand. Give him, too, this golden mace, and say to him that so soon as he hath come to do me homage I will march against Charlemagne. And if the Emperor will not kneel at my feet asking mercy and if he will not deny the Christian faith, I will tear his crown from his head!' 'Thy will shall be done,' answered the barons and, leaping upon their horses, they sped towards Saragossa.

Meanwhile, King Marsil, who had been seriously wounded by Roland, when he cut off his right hand in battle, and with such critical wounds fled the Roncesvalles Pass back to Saragossa. His servants were shocked to see their master return in such a sorry state. His broken sword, his shattered helmet and chest armour he gave to them. Then he flung himself down upon the grass hiding his face, and there in the shadow of an olive tree, he seemed to breathe his last breath.

When the Queen Bramimonde heard that her lord had returned, she hurried to him. Then seeing him lying there with a shattered wrist, from which the right hand was gone, she wept aloud and made a great moan. With terrible curses she cursed Charlemagne and France, she cursed her heathen gods and idols. Then she threw the image of Apollo down, taking from him his crown and sceptre and trampling him underfoot. 'Oh, wicked god,' she cried, 'why hast thou brought such shame upon us? Why hast thou allowed our king to be defeated? Thou rewards' will be a curse upon those e who serve thee.'

As the messengers of Baligant, the Emir and his knights came near to the city they heard a great noise. It was the heathen folk who wept and cried and made great moans, cursing their gods and Muhammad who had done naught for them. 'Miserable beings that we are,' they cried, 'what will become of us?' Shame and misfortune have fallen upon us. We have lost our king, for Roland hath cut off his right hand. His fair son too is dead. All Spain is in the hands of the Franks.'

The Emir's messengers returned to him telling him that he had been wounded to death. There they told Baligant all they had heard. " and if you go to the King now in his final hour, he swears to give you the whole of Spain and he will do this on a handshake unto his last breath. So it was that the King commanded his servants to 'Raise him' when he saw Baligant, the Emir approaching. Then taking his glove in his left hand he gave it to the Emir. 'Lord Baligant' he said: 'With this glove, I give you all my lands. I am henceforth thy vassal, for I am lost, all my people are lost.'. 'Thy grief is great,' said Baligant, 'and I cannot speak long with thee, for Charlemagne expects me not, and I must hasten to take him unawares. But I accept thy glove since thou giveth it to me.' Then, glad at the thought of possessing all of Spain, Baligant seized the glove. Quickly he ran down the steps, sprang upon his horse, and was soon spurring back to his army. 'Forward, forward,' he cried, 'the Franks cannot now escape us.'

And thus it was that as Charlemagne had made an end of burying the dead heroes, and was ready to depart homeward, a great noise of trumpets and shouting, of clang and clatter of armour and neighing of horses came to his ear. Soon over the hills appeared the glitter of helmets, and two messengers from the heathen army came spurring towards the Emperor. 'Proud King, thou canst no longer escape,' they cried. 'Baligant the Emir is here, and with him is a mighty army. Today we will see if thou art truly valorous.' Charlemagne tore at his beard, looking darkly at the messengers. Then drawing himself up, he threw a proud look over his army. In a loud and strong voice, he cried, 'To horse, my barons, to horse and arms.'

Such was Charlemagne's answer to the prideful message of the Emir. For he was the first to arm, and when his Franks soldiers saw him ride before them with his glittering helmet and shield, and his sword Joyeuse girt about him, they cried aloud, 'Such a man was made indeed to wear a crown.'Then calling to him two of his best knights, Charlemagne gave to them, one the sword of Roland, the other his ivory horn. 'Ye shall carry them,' he said, 'at the head of all the army.' And when the trumpets sounded to battle, louder and sweeter than them all sounded the horn of Roland.

Rustichello, upon reading this had a moment of clarity about Roland's sword Durangal and its magic powers, for here was written proof that Emperor Charlemagne had given both the sword and the Oliphant horn to two of his favoured warrior knights to use as banners in leading the battle charge. So whose sword was it that was embedded in the rocky cliff face tab the death of Roland in Roncesvalles Pass? It seems he had more research to do on that subject of the word if he was to recover the real sword for his employer, King Phillip 111. The answer to this riddle would be revealed to him on his return journey on the Camino at the Monastery of Roncesvalles.

In the thickest of the fight, the Emperor and the Emir met. Then a fearful fight took place. Blow upon blow fell, sparks flew and again and again, the two knights charged, and wheeled and charged anew. Such were the shocks, that at last their saddle girths broke and both were thrown to the ground. Quickly Charlemagne and Balignat the Emir sprang up again and renewed the fight on foot. 'Think, Charlemagne,' cried, the Emir, as they fought, 'ask pardon of me and promise to be my vassal, and I will give thee all Spain and the East.' 'I owe neither peace nor love to a heathen,' replied Charlemagne. 'Become a Christian, and I will love thee henceforth.''I would rather die,' answered the Emir. So they fought on. With a mighty blow, the Emir broke Charlemagne's helmet and wounded him sorely on the head. Emperor Charlemagne staggered and almost fell, and it seemed as if his strength went from him. But his guardian angel whispered to him, 'Great King, what doest thou?' And when Charlemagne heard the angel whisper, his strength came to him anew, and with one great blow, he laid the Emir dead at his feet. Then the Emperor remembered his dream of a victory over a lion that had attacked him and knew that the victory was to him and that the Emir was the lion who attacked him in his dream. As to the heathen, when they saw their leader fall, they fled. Terrible was the slaughter and the chase. Through the heat and dust of the day, the Franks pursued the fleeing heathen, even to the walls of Saragossa.

There in a high tower sat Queen Bramimonde, praying with her heathen priests for the victory of the Emir. But when she looked forth from her tower and saw the heathen ride in dire confusion, chased by the victorious Franks, she broke out again into loud wailing. Running to King Marsil she cried, 'Oh, noble King, our men are beaten. We are undone.' Then Marsil, in utter grief, turned his face to the wall and died.

Now to the very gates of the palace, the noise of battle came. The streets of the town were full of armed men, pursuing and pursuing. And before night fell all the city was in the hands of Charlemagne. The Franks entered every heathen temple and broke the graven images into pieces. Then all the heathen were baptized, and those who would not become Christian were put to death. Such was the way in those fierce old times. Leaving a garrison to guard the town, Charlemagne set forth for France once more, leading with him captive Queen Bramimonde. At Blaye, upon the shores of the Gironde, the three heroes, Roland, Oliver, and Archbishop Turpin were buried with great pomp and ceremony, and after long journeying the Emperor arrived at last at his great city of Aix. Then from all the corners of his kingdom, he gathered his wise men to judge the traitor Ganglion.

Then Charlemagne, The emperor sat upon his throne with all his wise men around him, and into the hall came Aude, the fair sister of Oliver. At the foot of the throne, she knelt. 'Sire,' she said, 'where is Roland, whose bride I am?' Full of grief the Emperor bent his head. Tears stood in his eyes, and at first, he could not speak. Then gently taking Aude by the hand, 'Dear sister,' he said, ', thou asked news of a dead man. But grieve not. Thou art not left without a lover. Thou shalt be the bride of Louis, my son.'

Then Aude stood up, her face was very pale. With both hands, she pushed back her golden hair from her face. 'What strange words are these?' she said. 'If Roland be dead, what is any man to me? Please God and His saints and angels, I too may die.' And so speaking she fell at the Emperor's feet. Charlemagne thought that she had but fainted, and springing up, he lifted her in his arms. But her head fell back upon her shoulder, and he saw that she was dead. Then calling four countesses he bade them carry her to a convent nearby. And so tended by the greatest ladies in the land, fair Aude was laid to rest with chant, hymn, and great state and pomp as befits a hero's bride.

Then, with chains upon his hands and feet, Ganglion was brought into the hall of judgment. Sitting upon his throne, the Emperor spoke to his wise men who were gathered around him and told them all the tale of Ganglion's treachery, and of how for gold he had betrayed his comrades. Proud and haughty as ever, Ganglion stood before his judges. 'It is true,' he said; 'I will never deny it. I hated Roland, for his riches made me wrathful against him. I sought to bring him to shame and death. But I do not admit that it was treason.' He also gave an account of a long battle that Roland had with a giant warrior of the Moors before he was overcome by him, but Charlemagne dismissed this as a lie.

'Of that, we shall be the judges,' said the Franks. Tall and straight and proud, Ganglion stood before the Emperor. With haughty looks he eyed his judges, and then his thirty kinsmen who stood near him. 'Hear me, barons,' he cried, in a bold, loud voice. 'When I was with the army of the Emperor, I served him in faith and love. But Roland his nephew hated me. He condemned me to death, yea, to a very miserable death, in sending me to the court of Marsil. That I escaped that death I owe to my skill. And I defied Roland, I defied Oliver and all his companions, before the face of Charlemagne and his barons. Well knew the Emperor of that defiance. It was just vengeance, then, that I took. Of no treason am I guilty?' 'We shall judge of that,' said the Franks. And so they passed into the council chamber. Then when Ganglion saw what it was like to go ill with him, he gathered his thirty kinsmen about him and begged them to plead for him. But it was chiefly in Pinabel, his nephew, that he trusted, for he was wise and could plead well, and as a good soldier, there was none like him. 'In thee do I trust,' said Ganglion, 'thou art he who must save me from death and shame.' 'I will be thy champion,' replied Pinabel. 'If any Frank say that thou art a traitor, I will give him the lie with the steel of my sword. Then Ganglion fell upon his knees and kissed Pinabel's hand.

And when all the wise men and barons were gathered together, Pinabel pleaded so well for Ganglion that at last, they said, 'Let us pray the Emperor to pardon Ganglion this once. Henceforward he will serve him in love and faith. Roland is dead. Not all the gold or all the silver in the world can bring him to life again. To fight about it, that is folly.'

Only one knight, called Thierry, would not agree. 'Ganglion is a traitor worthy of death,' he said. But the others would not listen to him, and they all returned to Charlemagne, to tell him what they had decided. 'Sire,' they said, 'we come to beg thee to set Ganglion free. He is a true knight, though this once he hath done ill he repents, and will henceforth serve thee in love and faith. Roland is dead, and not all the gold or silver in the world can bring him back again.'

When the Emperor heard these words, his face grew dark with anger. 'Ye are all felons,' he cried. Then dropping his head upon his breast, 'Unhappy man that I am,' he moaned, 'to be thus forsaken of all.'Out of the crowd stepped Thierry. He was slim and slight, but very knightly to look upon. 'Sire,' he cried, 'thou art not forsaken of all. By my forefathers, I have a right to be among the judges in this cause. What quarrel lay between Roland and Ganelion hath naught to do with this. Ganelion, I say, is a felon. Ganelion is a traitor. Ganelion is a liar. Let him be hanged and his body thrown to the dogs. Such is the punishment of traitors. And if any of his kin say I lie, I am ready to prove the truth of my words with my good sword which hangs by my side.' "Well, spoken! well spoken!' cried the Franks.

Then before Emperor Charlemagne, Pinabel advanced. He was tall and strong and with his sword most skilful. 'Sire,' he cried, 'there is the right to decide this cause. Thierry hath dared to judge in it. I say he lies. Battle thereon will I do,' and so speaking he flung his glove on the ground. 'Good,' said Charlemagne, well pleased. 'But I must have hostages. Thirty of Ganelion's kinsmen shall be held in the prison ward until this jousting is done.'

Then Thierry drew off his glove and gave it to the Emperor. For him also thirty hostages were held in the prison ward until it should be seen who should have right in this quarrel. Beyond the walls of Aix, there was a fair meadow, and there the champions met. All around there were seats set so that the knights and barons might look on, and in the middle of them was Charlemagne's throne. The champions were both clad in new and splendid armour, the trumpets sounded, and springing to the horse they dashed upon each other. Fiercely they fought. Their shields were dinted by many a blow, their armour battered and broken, and at last, they met with such a shock that both were unhorsed and fell to the ground.

'Oh, Heaven!' cried Charlemagne, 'show me which hath right.' Then he remembered his dream of the bear and his thirty brethren, and of how the hound from out his palace hall had grappled with the greatest of them. Both knights sprang lightly from their fall and began to fight on foot. 'Yield thee, Thierry,' cried Pinabel, 'and I will henceforth be thy man and serve thee in faith and love. All my treasure will I give to thee, if thou but pray the Emperor to forgive Ganelion.' 'Never,' cried Thierry, 'shame be to me should I think thereon. Let God decide between me and thee this day.' So they fought on. 'Then Pinabel,' said Thierry presently, 'thou art a true knight. Thou art tall and strong, and all men know of thy courage, so yield thee, and make thy peace with Charlemagne. As to Ganelion, let justice be done on him, and let us never more speak his name.'

'Nay,' replied Pinabel, 'God forbid that I should so forsake my kinsman, and to mortal man, I will never yield. Rather let me die than earn such disgrace.' So once again they chose the fight. Thicker and faster fell the blows. Their chain mail was hacked to pieces. The jewels of their helmets sparkled on the grass. Thierry was wounded in the face. Blood blinded him, but raising his sword with all his remaining strength, he brought it crashing down on Pinabel's helmet. For a moment the knight waved his sword wildly in the air. Then he fell to the ground dead. The fight was over. 'Now by the judgment of God, is it proved that Ganelion is a traitor,' cried the Franks. 'He deserves to be hanged, both he and all his kindred who have answered for him.' And as all the people cheered the champion of Roland's cause, Charlemagne rose from his throne, and going to him took him in his arms and kissed him, and threw his royal mantle around his shoulders. Then very tenderly his squires disarmed the wounded knight, set him upon a gently pacing mule, and led him back in triumph to Aix.

Once again Charlemagne called all his wise men and barons together. 'What shall be done with the hostages who pled for Ganelion?' he asked.

'Let them all die the death,' replied the Franks.

Then the Emperor called an old provost to him. 'Go,' he said, 'hang them all on the gallows there. And if one escape, by my long white beard, thou shalt die the death.' 'None shall escape,' replied the provost, 'trust me.' Then taking with him a hundred sergeants he hanged the thirty high upon the gallows tree. But a still more fearful death was to be the fate of the traitor Ganelion himself. Bound hand and foot, he was led through the town riding upon a common cart horse, while the people cursed him as he passed. And beyond the walls, where his champion had fought and died for him, he was torn to pieces by wild horses.

So Rustichello da Pisa, after reading of the seven-year war battles of Charlemagne against the hearth Moors, the death of Roland in the song of Roland fable, his mystical magic sword Durendal and his Oliphant horn in which he blew so hard he burst his temples and his eardrums, at the point of death at the Roschevalles Pass, and of the betrayal and fate of the Ganelion, believed he had enough information as to understand more readily his mission of the three tasks he must complete in the next six weeks in the name of the king'..

Rustichello, a well-read man of faith and deeds of action, despite his wife's betrayal, his broken heart and financial misfortune took upon himself the mission assigned to him by the King. For well he knew he would need the variety of his talents to fulfil the mission. And so it was that Rustichello da Pisa, the Master of the Arts, presented himself to King Phillip111 on his final instruction before venturing on the Camino Way, to firstly do penance for the sin of his king by presenting a bag of gold at the altar of St.James where his remains reportedly lay, thenceforth to journal his daily activities, observations and mysteries of The Way, taking in particular an account of Moor troops and fortifications on the Camino, but not journalling his findings; instead commenting those to memory in thus reporting back to his king on his return to the Castle from which he was about to depart.

In addition, he had been instructed to take the low route on the return journey across the Pyrenees, staying overnight in the Monastery at Roncesvalles and the very next day make his way to the pass where Roland had been slayed. It was his sworn duty there to extract Durendal, the mystical sword of Roland and at the king's wish to deliver it to him. Whilst King Philip knew that it was a near-impossible task to complete, he never-theless had delivered this to Rustichello as part of his instruction for the pilgrimage.

CHAPTER 3.

THE WAY OF RUSTICHELLO

Rustichello, having read extensively on the necessities for his pilgrimage had carefully packed his knapsack carrying but one change of clothing for day and night wear, a small quantity of fruit, a mixed variety of nuts and three kilos of water to quench his thirst along The Way. All in all, he estimated he should carry no more than ten per cent of his body weight but for good measure added a small sleeping bag and a tent just in case he was left outside to the dangers of elements on the mountain's terrain. Once the King had supplied him with a purse of gold to cover the expense of his mission, the bag of gold nuggets, the burden of weight that he must carry in retribution for the sin of his king, to be for delivery to Compostela de Santiago and placed at the foot of the tomb of St James, under the altar at the Cathedral, the pilgrim realised his pack could be extra difficult over the eight hundred mile journey to Santiago.

Then the King added a gift to Rustichello, the Codex Calixtinus, a recent illuminated manuscript formerly attributed to Pope Callixtus II, that had been arranged by the French scholar Aymeric Picaud. The King explained to Rustichello that the principal author was given the task of 'Scriptwriter' And the work was intended as an anthology of background detail and advice for pilgrims following the Way of St. James to the shrine of the apostle Saint James the Great, located in the cathedral of Santiago de Compostela, Galicia. The King added: "The Codex Calixtinus is alternatively known as the Liber Sancti Jacobi or the Book of Saint James. The collection includes sermons, reports of miracles and liturgical texts associated with Saint James, and a most interesting set of polyphonic musical pieces. In it are also found descriptions of the route, works of art to be seen along the way, and the customs of the local people."

King Phillip, a most well-read man of letters himself, had come to believe the Codex may have been written by several different authors and then compiled as a single volume, possibly between 1135 and 1139 by the French scholar Picaud. Whilst it is said to have the authority of Pope Callixtus II, it is thought that to lend authority to their work, the authors prefaced the book with a forged letter purportedly signed by the Pope who at the time had already died in 1124.

So on this day in 1270, Rustichello made his way from the kingdom of Philip 111, newly appointed king of France, on the horseback of the best of the King's horses bound for St. Jean Pied de Port, where he was to leave the horse with a stable hand that had already received instructions from a King's messenger of the arrival of a pilgrim on a mission for his majesty. So it was that Rustichello made haste to ride the day journey to a place not far from St Jean to commence a journey on foot to ascent on the Pyrenees mountains, overburdened by a backpack of basic needs, a sleeping bag., a tent that he wondered if he was really in need of, a purse of gold for his keep, a bag of nuggets as a burden representing his King's sin and now a copy of the original Codex Calixtinus of which he now knew the original documents were now held in the archives of the Cathedral of Santiago de Compostela and dated from about 1150. His copy he noted was of the Santiago edition and was made in 1173 by the monk Arnaldo de Monte, known as The Ripoll after the monastery of Santa Maria de Ripoll in Catalonia.

Rustichello, realising that he was carrying an overweight pack of at least five kilos was already figuring out what to jettison before he commenced. He laid out the contents of his pack before repacking, to see what he could leave behind to lighten his load. He noted that the cloth parcel given to him by his King had the compiled Codex Calixtinus the same as The Santiago de Compostela copy comprises five volumes, totalling 225 double-sided folios each with some 295 pages and more with some exceptions, each folio displays a single column of thirty-four lines of text 4 mm. apart. The pilgrim began to evaluate the need for each book but took it upon himself to absorb all five books' contents.

The Master of the Arts noted that Book I accounted for almost half of the volumes and contained sermons and homilies concerning Saint James, two descriptions of his martyrdom and official liturgies for his veneration. Its relative size and the information it contains on the spiritual aspects of the pilgrimage make it the heart of the codex. The hagiographic Book II took account of twenty miracles across Europe attributed to Saint James, both during his life and after his death. It was noted that the recipients and witnesses of these miracles were often pilgrims. Rustichello remembered reading of the many miracles of Christ during the years before his death on the cross for mankind's sin and after he had risen from the dead. He noted in memory that James had equally performed miracles of great amazement to his Jesus the Savour. Rustichello then remembered the word of the son of man   to his apostles: "And greater miracles than these will you perform also, for, you will do them in my name."

Rustichello then turned to the book entitled Liber de translatio corporis sancti Jacobi ad Compostellam a religious translation of St James of the Compostela; Book III is a brief of the five books and describes the transfer of Saint James' body from Jerusalem to his tomb in Galicia. It also tells of the custom started by the first pilgrims to gather souvenir sea shells from the Galician coast. The scallop shell is a symbol of Saint James. So then Rustichello turned to volume Book IV attributed to Archbishop Turpín of Reims. There he noted an annotation that, although the work is of an anonymous writer of the 12th century, it describes the coming of Charlemagne to Spain, his defeat at the Battle of Roncevaux Pass and the death of the knight Roland. It relates how Saint James then appeared in a dream to Charlemagne, urging him to liberate his tomb from the Moors and showing him the direction to follow by the route of the Milky Way. This association has given the Milky Way an alternate name in Spain of Camino de Santiago. The chapter also includes an account of Roland's defeat of the giant Saracen Ferragut. This widely publicized and multi-copied book describes the legend of Santiago Matamoros or 'St. James the Moorslayer' is considered by scholars to be an early example of propaganda by the Catholic Church to drum up recruits for the military Order of Santiago. The Order was formed to help protect church interests in northern Spain from Moorish invaders. Rustichello, read now on the subject of the death of Roland, and the battles of Charlemagne and in later years the legend became somewhat of an embarrassment in its depiction of Saint James as a bloodthirsty avenger 800 years after his death.

King Philip III had ordered that Book IV be removed from the codex and for a while, it circulated as a separate volume but the King had thought it fitting to give Rustichello his copy. Rustichello was soon to find on his pilgrimage throughout northern Spain along the Way of St. James known as the Camino Frances, most churches and cathedrals still had a sanctuary and chapels applauding 'Saint James the Moor slayer'.

Rustichello was thankful to the King for Book V for it housed a wealth of practical advice for pilgrims, informing them where they should stop, relics they should venerate, sanctuaries they should visit, and commercial scams and bad food they should be wary of. The book provided him with valuable insight into the life of the 12th-century pilgrim. It also describes the city of

Santiago de Compostela and its cathedral. It would follow in time a popular appeal of Book V that led to it achieving the greatest fame, and history would prove it to be described as the first tourist's guidebook. Among Basque scholars, this account was to be considered highly important because it contains some of the earliest Basque words and phrases of the post-Roman period.

As Rustichello repacked his pack a parchment paper with a handwritten note fell from Book V It said The Camino or The Way lies directly under The Milky Way and follows key ley (energy) lines that reflect the energy from the stars above. In Eastern philosophies, the spiritual life force (prana) is inextricably linked with the life force of the sun and is especially strong along lines of energy called ley lines. This is in turn linked to the energies conducted within our galaxy, other galaxies and the star systems. The Camino that follows the earth's ley lines begins in France, at St. Jean-Pied-de-Port, and makes its way east to west across The Pyrenees to the famous cathedral called Santiago de Compostela, in Santiago, where the remains of St. James the Greater, the apostle of Jesus are said to be interred.

And so Rustichello read on from some pilgrim journalling: I determined to adopt an accord of consciousness with every human being with whom I would come in contact on my outward and inward journey: a journey of understanding; a journey of nature being both cruel and kind; of being as vigilant as a female serpent within my inner being on the pathways of my life, and as innocent as a dove. A freedom nothing bar death could take from me – my freedom of choice for living. I knew within my heart of hearts there existed a Sword of Discernment and I longed for an outward expressive symbol of this inner need and courage. I would venture forth, to let go of my inner turmoil and take a journey of the spirit – my spiritual heart expressed in a real symbol. I could think of no better way than the way of St. James, the apostle, whose symbol was a real Sword of Discernment; the sacrificial cross of St. James, the fleury fitch, whose sword blade signifies the sword of a warrior. I would follow the path of St. James, The Moorslayer, on The Camino Way, where I would lay down my burdens and walk the traditional Way that so many pilgrims had walked before me.

It was the note of a pilgrim about to begin his Camino journey of The Way just like Rustichello himself was about to venture and a reminder to journal every day his own experiences of a mental, physical and spiritual nature, for he felt at that time he needed to release his burdens along The Way of walking out of darkness and into some new light of existence. It was not just for the King then that he began to walk The Way.

Rustichello was determined more than ever to have a better understanding of his journey by reading the five volumes more closely before he walked past the first marker of The Way. So it was that the pilgrim noted:

'The Association of James as the patron saint of Spain has no basis in the bible but exists only in the realm of tradition, oral history, legend and myth. The story that St. James preached that faith without works is dead, meaning that actions speak louder than words. He was not very successful, recruiting only seven disciples during his seven years of preaching in Spain. The last we hear of James is in the biblical account of his martyrdom at the hands of Herod Agrippa in Rome, in about 44 CE (Acts 22:12).

The legend says that James' body was transported to Spain on a stone ship without oars or sail, Viking-style, carried by angels and the wind. The ship landed at Iria Flavia and James' disciples met the ship there and carried his body to a nearby hill where he was buried. The body of James appears to have been forgotten for the next seven-and-a-half centuries, until 813. It is written that a Christian hermit named Pelayo saw, on Mount Libredon, a shining light that led him to James' grave and the remains of two of James' disciples, Atanasio and Teodoro. The bishop authenticated the relics and, to honour the Saint, King Alfonso II built a chapel that drew a modest number of pilgrims. The Cathedral de Santiago was commenced in 1075 and completed in 1120. It is reported that below the main altar in the cathedral, the remains of St. James are encased in a tomb, and pilgrims have flocked there ever since to pay homage.'

The scallop shell remains the symbol of the Camino, its outer shell representing the many routes that lead to Santiago. The shell has been used for centuries to denote that an individual displaying it is on a pilgrimage and is protected. Historically, the Knights Templar of the Order of St. James, whose symbol is a red sword, protected pilgrims on The Camino Way against thieves and vagabonds. The Camino de Santiago may seemingly be a Christian experience, but many people of other faiths, or no faith at all, walk the path, as in those Medieval times.

A myth about the modest shrine of St. James recounts the battle of Clavijo, where the Spanish fought the Muslim invaders. James is said to have appeared, arriving on a white horse with the sword of the Templars above his head, leading the Spanish into battle. The image of St. James was a convenient motif to draw Christian support to the frontier of the Muslim-Christian battle and to bolster financial support for the Christian domination of Iberia.

It is said that the Christian soldiers scattered some of James' ashes during the battle, whilst the Muslims had a mummified arm of Mohammed in a cloth as a guiding symbol. Although the fact that the legend lives on that James appeared on the battlefield at Clavijo, seems to be a direct consequence of the Christians regaining the upper hand in Spain, it is merely a story. St. James, as the best of scholars seem to agree, never came to Spain. There is no earthly reason why his body should have been brought to Galicia and nothing is suggested in the Acts of the Apostles in the bible, where his death is recorded. James died several centuries before Islam was conceived, probably never mounted a horse in his life and certainly never slew a Muslim. There is no earthly reason why Santiago should be a place of pilgrimage, although it is.

Rustichello was reading his journal notes from the first day of his Camino before heading off to the monastery dormitory at Roncesvalles to sleep. Starting along The Way, I awoke to the hot morning sun pouring into my attic haven. I quickly washed and headed to a nearby inn for a hearty breakfast. The temperature was already high as I paid the innkeeper for his hospitality and made my way outside, but had not filled my water ghoul from the water jug on the table but I did stuff another bread roll into my backpack for the journey ahead.

Those of us of older vintage hang about the edges of our heart's desires, scarred by the world of reality over a lifetime of living within linear rational faith, and find ourselves on The Camino determined to let go of our long-held burdens, with some hope of either regaining the innocence of the Christian belief of our youth or hoping to experience a renewal of our former faith. I was of the latter, hoping to let go of the burdens of my heart and looking to experience some former Catholic doctrine of faith and morals by visiting ancient church buildings and attending religious services along the way.

I was hoping to embrace the passion, wildness and enthusiasm of my youth, in a last-ditch effort to hold on to whatever youth was left in me. This was an intricate part of my search on The Camino, my last hurrah before I resigned myself to the inevitable realisation of letting go of the youth that I once was but was no longer.

I meandered my way out of the village of St. Jean-Pied-de-Port, already feeling the perspiration trickle down my back in the forty-degree heat. It was mid-morning and I was the only pilgrim heading to the foothills of The Pyrenees at that time. A yellow arrow marker on a milestone of rock pointing the way, the ultimate signpost for me as my introduction to The Camino Way.

The climb up the ancient well-traversed French Way continued steeply to five hundred metres and, despite the heat, gave me pause to view the valley below and beyond to the now-distant view of St. Jean-Pied-de-Port; as I continued my climb, the village slowly vanished behind me. The heavy backpack was already taking its toll, but with determination, I continued the climb in the blistering heat. I was beginning to realise that, I had no need of the tent for this journey, and regretted that I had not left it behind. Here and there along the track pilgrims had jettisoned unwanted items of clothing, including boots, jackets, hats and towels, and personal memorabilia. Near a point called Orison, eight hundred metres up, I came across a shrine where pilgrims had left rosary beads, caps, bracelets, business cards, a journal and a manuscript. Either this was the first stage of letting go of material possessions or an indication that some found the going tough and left some of the weight from their backpacks at this popular dumping ground. The shrine had some Christian religious symbolism and was surrounded by a wrought-iron enclosure, so it was a sign to let go of something related to material possessions or bad habits.

The Camino scallop shell and markers denote the many roads throughout Europe that ultimately converge as one, not far from the city of Leon. The back of the shell appears like a map, with the ridges all coming to a central point on the edge of the shell. Apart from being the main signposting along the route to Santiago, it has another symbolic meaning: it is said that when you turn the shell over, it resembles an open hand of kindness. Most of what I was to encounter on my Camino would prove to me that the shell carried on pilgrims' backpacks to denote that were on a pilgrimage should have been worn inside-out. If pilgrims knew in advance, they may have considered it a symbolic gesture, or invitation if you will, to show mercy to the many beggars and unemployed youth encountered in the cities and villages on the journey to Santiago. At that, Rustichello put his quill, ink and journal in his pack content that he had recorded something for his king and then he fell into a deep sleep. Rustichello was awakened with a bright light in his eyes, and unable to get back to sleep again for some time he lit a candle and began to write up his journal

Rustichello rose to finish writing up his account of the previous day's journey The climb to Lepoeder, on the way to Roncesvalles, was a total of seventeen kilometres and almost 1,500 metres up. It was then a slow-walking steep fall for the next ten kilometres to the cosy Medieval hamlet of Roncesvalles Walking on a cobblestone pathway under an archway, I encountered the Conventus Hospitalis Roncesvalles for my first stay at an albergue, or pilgrim's hostel or refugio, on The Camino. The volunteer hospital greeted me with an official "Hullo" and requested my Crecencial el Peregrino, the passport allowing a pilgrim to use The Camino system of accommodation, which, when stamped, is documented proof that a pilgrim has completed the journey. It provides the right of entry into all Albergues on The Camino. The completed passport is necessary for claiming the Compostela certificate, evidence that the entire distance to Santiago has been completed. So he purchased his pilgrim's passport from the Hosptalis.' desk marking it as beginning from Jean-Pied-de-Port before adding her official Roncesvalles stamp. He could now officially call himself a pilgrim.

Rustichello began to walk the once blood-stained valley where Charlemagne returned to find his beloved nephew dead. After about an hour he reached the main pathway to Santiago and, at the junction, was a busy little oasis café. Like so many other pilgrims he crowded into the small provision store for some fruit, biscuits and milk, as this was the first and only opportunity to eat some breakfast. The food was not very nourishing, but it was better than walking with an empty stomach he surmised.

It was whilst he sat eating the not-so-wholesome food that Rustichello decided to write snippets only of his pilgrimage so as not to bore the king to tears on his return journey. to the French palace in Paris He started a new page beginning with ' To my King. So as not to put you to sleep with excessive words I resolve now to enter only the broad facts of the matters that I take the liberty of assuming you will be appreciative of for the remainder of this Camino'. But he felt himself at liberty to write an ecological point to his current human condition

King Gougia, in the magnum opus of the ancient Chinese of the 5th century CE, was captured by his arch-enemy and made to suffer three years imprisonment before being given amnesty. Rather than return to his throne, he resolved to eat peasant food and live simply. He slept on a bed of brushwood and licked a gallbladder every day to taste life's bitterness. It was, for him, a reminder of the shame and humiliation he had suffered in captivity, and he drew strength from it. The memory of that story bolstered my spirits; I believed that I could, for most of the day, live off the mal-nourishment I had just consumed, but did wonder how my energy could be maintained in the now sweltering heat.

And so he continued with his journalling It proved to be a beautiful day for walking and meeting many more new pilgrims on their life journeys on the Camino. The pathway, at about 1,000 metres above sea level, remained easygoing for the majority of the 23.3 km to Zubiri. There, he planned for the day to end and to find a peaceful way to relax. The forested walking trails and occasional river crossings were a welcome change after the Pyrenees crossing of the previous day. The day's trek was often broken by walking through charming little villages, which seemed to ease the burden of thinking about the heaviness of his overweight backpack.

Rustichello was relieved to take the backpack off about halfway through the day and, whilst resting in the shade of an old oak tree, enjoyed the remainder of the food he had purchased in a café in a village he had passed through. Here and there the path that he was taking was marked with red and white striped arrows. As he got closer to Zubiri, the arrows indicating the direction changed to yellow and blue. Then they changed again, rainbow colours slowly melted to more yellow shells and yellow arrows; yellow being the traditional colour of The Camino.

It was dusk when he arrived at Zubiri, but there were no immediate signs of accommodation, so he headed for a café for a drink and food, and once again was greeted by recently-met pilgrims. There he stayed awhile for a second drink before bidding them the Camino farewell and continuing along the road to find a room for the night. He could not find anywhere to stay along the pathway, so resolved to keep walking, as there was still plenty of daylight. The oppressive heat and the now broken blisters on both feet proved to be irritating and painful, and he was beginning to regret that he had not searched a little harder for accommodation in Zubiri. Still, the pathway looked safe enough and he could easily have pitched his tent and made camp for the night. However, he resolved to soldier on, despite the discomfort of wearing too-thick socks in the hot conditions and the constant movement of feet in his boots rubbing like sandpaper on raw blisters. It occurred to him that he would have been far better off following the nearby Arga River, meandering along its banks through rural hamlets on a pleasant nature pathway to Pamplona.

Rustichello figured he would reserve the remaining 21 km to Pamplona for that purpose tomorrow and, despite his discomfort, walked the remaining 6 km of the traditional way to Akerreta to find a bed for the night. He did finally secure an inn for his night's rest. In the diary entry, he just jotted down the distance walked in the heat, named a pilgrim or two that he had met and noted the word " No Moors.' for his later report to the king. This was to be the pattern of his daily journal of The Way, except to go into greater detail on the myths legends and folklore of his Camino de Santiago and write a poem or two for the king's pleasure. He then begins to write of the universal man as he sees him on this Camino Way.

CHAPTER 4

WORDS IN A JOURNAL

"We, the people of this earth, black, white, red and yellow on an orca-white background coloured in the clouds of the rainbow spirit, of the spirit of the bright moon, of the blazing sun, of the red earth, of the dark earth, the rivers, the waters, the plants and the animals, and of the Dreamtime, the descendants of song-lines and painted images on cave walls. We are the present-day images of the Gods we believe in collectively and individually, of the one true creator, of the manifestation of a Son, a holy Higher Self or spirit linked to the Creator God, the Father of all Fathers, the ghost who exists as a pale reflection of ourselves as we gaze into small ponds.

We are the wandering man who goes walkabout in the deserts, in dreamtime with the Creator. We are the red man who sits in a teepee tent smoking a peace pipe, in touch with his ancestors in the black hills of Dakota, negro man of Africa offering a sacrificial prayer to his God, the Jewish man with a sacrificial lamb, the white man of sacrificial Christ, the Buddhists who meditate into their spirituality, the adherents of Islam who believe in a Mohammed of the desert. Such are this world's manifestations that are meant to bring peace not war, to encourage wise men to make amends for wrongdoing, to progress forward into the light and not return to the darkness; these are the myths, legends and folklore that will make this generation and future generations all the better for continuing our respective beliefs. We have but to give in meditating on our feelings and emotions, bringing them into line by handing over to a Higher Power belief or manifested disbelief without much thought. Just by doing this in peaceful calm seems to penetrate our very beings and we are on a different plane."

I arrived at an albergue in the centre of town near the river at around 9:00 pm and proceeded to the reception after waiting a good ten minutes before the door was opened for me. The male receptionist abruptly demanded my Camino passport, stamped it and waited impatiently while I fumbled for the coin charge for my bed for the night. He led me up a staircase and, in a mix of Spanish and English, showed me around. He took me to the lockers to secure my backpack, wallet and boots. It took another trip downstairs for a further charge for the locker before I had both the front door key and locker key in my possession.

The Albergue was practically empty, so I had a quick shower, changed my clothing and headed off to a nearby bar, which was the only place still open in this town. I managed to convince the bartender to provide me with some leftovers from the kitchen, resulting in a bowl of soup and some bread. This place was thick with flies, already heading to the cool indoors. I ate my soup, dipping the remaining bread before eating, despite the flies crawling all over it. I simply didn't care, as it was good to get food into my stomach before falling asleep a few hours later in the Albergue. It had been a long and hard road of inner discovery, but I doggedly resolved to keep on keeping on. It was a pain-filled climax to the end of a day of walking 30 km.

Rustichello ceased writing the journal for the benefit of his King's later reading, so he put down the quill and returned to contemplation in the early morning light before venturing back to the Camino Way track. He had determined that he would write part of his journal for the king to read and understand. It would assist him in the remission of his sin when he finally delivered the gold nuggets to Santiago de Compostela's crypt off St. James, The Moor Slayer. He also felt the need to write about his inner feelings of pain and suffering. So he began to write a separate journal with the realisation that the Camino Way was not just a spiritual journal, but a journey of the spirit, his soul trek too.

He turned to the back of the journal and wrote down a series of subject matter for his later consideration. He divided it into columns for future reference purposes. The subject matter, another for feelings related to the seven deadly sins as dictated in the Bible, then a column for the matters relating to others, and a comments column for the part he played in past outcomes, as to whether he felt he had done all that he could to rectify the matters and make amends where appropriate.

He commenced by heading up the most pressing matters that had been disturbing him. First came the matter of his wife leaving him for another, then a column for the death of his precious son by his (own) hand, a column for the death of a friend, another for his folly present and past, and at that he paused to consider, then thinking that all matters deserved much thought before proceeding any further with journalling, so he turned back to recording his journal for the king.

At least today was going to be easier and, noted as I exited the town that the signpost indicated 15.4 km to Pamplona. I looked forward to taking it slow and steady on my sore feet and wounded, bound toes, arriving in the old city in the mid-afternoon. Sometimes I walked alone during this day and sometimes with other pilgrims en route, following the well-worn natural pathways. I often stopped for water which was in plentiful supply in purpose-built fountains intended for use by passing pilgrims. The distance across flat land on cobblestone, dirt and meadow green fields seems to pass quickly Rustichello put quill and the parchment journal book back in his backpack and didn't recommence writing until he was well into the midst of the city of Pamplona. later he returned to his journal:

The city was very crowded with tourists all lined up at the tourist van in the middle of the main square, looking for directions to monuments, accommodation and eateries and relaxing after witnessing the spectacle of the running of the bulls. I should have been aware that the city would be busy at this time of celebration.

St. Fermin, one of the many venerated saints of Pamplona, is the co-patron of Navarre, the autonomous country bordering the Basque mountains that I had just traversed. Pamplona, the capital of Navarre, is where the Saint Fermin Feast is celebrated, and the home of the running of the bulls. St. Fermin had been converted to Christianity and baptised by Saturnius, the bishop of Toulouse when Spain was under French rule. Saturnius and Fermin suffered martyrdom by being tied by the feet to a bull and dragged to their death. The three-day holiday celebration is an annual Pamplona event, but other towns and villages repeat the running of the bulls celebration long after Pamplona returns to normality.

Rustichello knew that the King was aware of the Moors' hold over the city and the betrayal of the head of state there in Charlemagne's time but he wrote this as a clue and a reminder to King Philip to read between the lines of dangers of another uprising in the region for these troubled times, for there were many Moor soldiers there enjoying the celebration. The Master of Arts returned to journaling: The city was in a celebratory mood and tourists were still hanging about, even though the running of the bulls was over. It meant I still had to carry my unwanted extra weight in my backpack for at least another 80 km; allowing for walking an average of 20 km per day, I would have to wait four more days.

The whole region of Navarre had stopped to celebrate the feast for the saint for days to come. In hindsight, I should have given all the extra-weight items to a local charity, but my childhood conditioning over-ruled the logic. I was educated to believe that hard work had earned me these things, and not to let go of them too easily. So my new-found motto in Spain, "Less is more on The Camino" failed me when it came to material possessions.

The exit from the city proved difficult, and he walked two or three kilometres in a jigsaw of crossroads and streets before he found the outskirts of the city. Whilst many official shell signs seemed to point in the right direction, many either faced the wrong way or were upside down, and sometimes even back the front to add to the confusion. He finally found his way to a stone milestone with a yellow arrow marker and was back on the Way again.

As Pamplona fades into the background, Rustichello begins the long ascent to the "hill of forgiveness", where the pilgrim statue at the "alto" is a timely reminder of the thousands who have walked this path for centuries. The 360-degree panoramic views of Pamplona and the valley ahead are sights to behold. The descent to Puente la Reina (Queen's Bridge) the Medieval alleys and the impressive 11th-century bridge over the River Arga are other wonders for the pilgrim. The Camino continues to the monuments of the Estella and the free wine fountain at the museum of Bodegas Irache.
Most of the walking passes vineyards, olive trees and cereal crops to Los Arcos. Here The Camino changes to the rolling countryside, where Rustichello leaves Navarre and enters the La Rioja region, famous for its red wines, passing from the dramatic ruins of Clavijo castle to the region's cap-

ital city of Logrono, known for the best of tapas and Rioja-style food specialties, a reward for the spirited master on his journey, and rest and recuperation after such a long but beautiful part of the Way.

The final exit from the city was by way of the Citadel Park, with views of the approaching climb to the small town of Cizur Memor. He stopped for a while, once again to rest his feet, there treating the blisters with honey and wrapping them in cloth. He had reached a small café after a relatively steep climb in the heat of the mid-morning, thankful for a break under a shaded awning. The place was crowded with many pilgrims, and Rustichello spoke to a young man from India who was attracted to the meditative movement of his Camino Way.

The climb up the steep slope to the wind-whipped Alto de Pardon was tough, but worth the effort. There I proceeded to draw pictures of the wonderful picturesque views of far-off mountain ranges and the closer, colourful valleys. Rustichello contented himself with writing a journal about the sights the day's sightings and his conversations with fellow pilgrims. He recorded in brief for the King rather than going into great detail and edited much from the reading.

The Medieval town of Alto de Pardon; consisted mainly of the Albergue. He had taken as sleeping quarters this quaint abode and had an enjoyable meal for the cost of a pittance. It was a welcome place for such an isolated location. This little town had once housed a basilica with a pilgrims' hospice and a hermitage. Now the only landmark was a row of some forty windmills standing on a nearby hilltop, providing electricity for the region

Rustichello had aimed to walk to Puente la Reina, a distance of 23.8 km from Pamplona, but had already covered some 18 km in the oppressive heat and felt that was far enough for the day. So, he decided to stay at an Albergue in the next village. The weight of his backpack was taking its toll in the blistering heat and the blisters on his feet were becoming a lot worse. He stayed the night at Camino de Pardon, which had a lovely eatery and a typical four-course meal, free wine for the drinkers, and ample bread, all for a total cost of only four deniers! He had exchanged a small gold nugget with a money lender for a livre which had been established by Charlemagne as a unit of account equal to one pound of silver. It was subdivided into 20 sols, and the four deniers were about a tenth of the value for his food and accommodation.

After a shower and further treatment of his blistered feet, Rustichello settled into bed for an early night with a final prayer before falling asleep, he had prayed that a carriage station would be open along the pathway, defying the saintly celebrations so that he could offload his tent and some of the possession he now felt unnecessary for the rest of the journey to Santiago. He deduced that they could transport them by carriage to Santiago for his later collection on arrival there.

Rustichello passed through Uterga before daybreak the next morning and heard the church bells ringing in the small nearby village of Obanos. The sight of the famous six-arched Romanesque bridge over the Rio Argo at Puenta la Reina came into view after a slow trudge by wheat fields and vineyards. The crops looked brown and parched from the dry Spanish summer. Crossing the bridge he remembered reading of how the town had grown around the bridge, which was built on the Santiago route so that pilgrims could avoid the ferrymen's expensive tariff, and also save them a treacherous boat ride. To his disappointment, everything in this town was closed for the anniversary celebrations.

The main street was busy with young people falling out of doorways, drunk from a night of wild dancing and red wine; all dressed in the same red shirts, black pants and red rags on their hips, mimicking the matadors of the historic arenas that once drew crowds to watch the matador kill the bull or vice versa. Rustichello climbed a fence to watch half-drunk young men attempting to fight a young bull in an enclosure in the square in the middle of the town. The small balconies that hung over the main square were filled with faces of old folk watching the antics of the alcohol-fuelled budding matadors. He was thankful to leave the street where the bulls would soon be released for the mad street dash in their running of the bulls celebration. Not as big a deal as the Pamplona celebrations, but still very dangerous all the same. Apart from his view of the stupidity of the young men in a drunken haze, he did not relish the thought of outrunning and fighting a bull with a red handkerchief. So Rustichello was quickly out of the street and back on The Camino Way.

The thought of my mantra, "Less is more on The Camino", played in his head as he left Estella in darkness, determined to make the 22 km to Los Argos by nightfall. The locals in Estella advised him that there would be no water for the next 12 km, so he wanted to get this part of the journey over before the temperature rose too high and yet another forty-degree day would have to be endured. It was a wise move, as without water and shade of which there were none, dehydration could result in a health crisis.

Rustichello had committed to memory the image of the rolling hills and vineyards at the halfway mark of Villa-mayor de Monjardin. The relief elicited a sigh from him when he sighted an imposing hilltop castle and entered the village square, seeing a free wine fountain in operation. His mind wandered back to letting go of painful experiences. For he knew that the inevitable battle with the Jewish moneylender for what was his rightful ownership of his possessions in Venice would be difficult unless he won favour with the King on his return. That would ensure his debts could be cleared and he would have some chance of living the life of a Merchant of Venice once more. He followed the column principles he had laid out in his journal and his conscious effort made amends in his heart for his indiscretions of being too fond of being a workaholic and enjoying the fruits of his labour instead of paying attention to his wife's needs of love and affection.

He recalled a message he had received before leaving Paris for the Camino, the death of his second eldest son by his hand For a time he felt a sense of abandonment from his family. The loss of material possessions had all taken a heavy toll on him. The stress resulted in a decline into depression and in the midst of all that, his mother's health failed, another friend suicided and another died. He had thought his life was over. Thankfully all this was now behind him, including the horror of being in a pit of hell whilst in the mindset of depression.

Like a meditative monk, he focused his efforts externally and his depression had lifted even before he left the King's castle and Paris. The focus was on research in the palace archives for the facts on the life of Charlemagne. The Story of Roland, the history behind the mystical sword Durandul, the somewhat mythical account of Roland's death and that of Ganelion's betrayal and death. Rustichello had also been focused on his packing and preparation for the Camino Way trek. So it came to pass that the depressed state of mind left him long before he began his initial climb up the Pyrenees mountains. Further, the release of his suffering heart came by writing his darkest poetry and entering the reasons behind his motives to make amends to all those he felt he needed to ask for pardon. He also realised that in most cases it made more sense just to write it all in his journal. He knew that he may just be opening up old wounds of a former life buried defects of others, and it was better to forgive and forget. He had but a simple rule of thumb in determining what he should or should not do. about his doubts. Firstly, did it trouble him and secondly, could he do anything about it if it did? If the answers to these questions were not a resounding 'Yes' the best thing to do was to just let it all go. He was in the right place for that. In his evaluation, the Camino was the place to let go of all things and just hand over to God. This was the philosophy of the journey.

Rustichello's mind returned to the road and the mental healing of The Camino de Santiago, his quest for King Philip and a motto that came to him in a dream: "Be as gentle as a dove and as vigilant as a female serpent." He realised that life needed to take the rough with the smooth. Thoughts of Buddha, Jesus and Mohammed came to him too. How they had suffered for their enlightenment. Avatars who knew the road to suffering led the way to enlightenment as his own Camino road journey now seemed to be doing for him.

The Camino is an inward journey, as well as an outward one. Whilst you meet many pilgrims along the road to Santiago, The Way is not so much a social experience, but more an experience of endurance, strength of character and soul-searching independence. As a pilgrim you get to know that the real task of your Camino is getting to know your physical endurance, and learning how to let go internally.

He jotted down an incident for the King's later amusement
After staying the night in Los Argos, I journeyed on a further 22 km that day, and a similar distance the next. The following day was not to be without incident. About nine kilometres from Logrono I noticed a make-shift sign with an arrow pointing to the left; the sign read, "Drink 1,000 metres". It was an extremely hot day and the thought of a cold drink enticed me to turn from the beaten Camino way and take a side dirt track to a small village on a hilltop. After quenching my thirst, I enquired as to another route back to The Camino Way, to save me from back-tracking the 1,000 metre path I had just walked. The Spanish guide directed me to another road, and when I came to a fork in the road I took the left turn as instructed.
At last, I came to a now familiar arrow painted on a large rock at the side of the track. The arrow on the rock pointed to a pathway at the edge of a vineyard and I began to walk along what I thought was the

correct route again but had not reckoned on the large arrow-marked rock having been moved in the wrong direction. After walking through the vineyards for a long time, I realised I was lost. I climbed to a high rocky ledge but could see no sign of life or a road, so I ventured on, not wanting to retrace my steps. After walking through a grassy field and a paddock full of burrs, I found a landmark; the meaning of the warning sign in Spanish was obvious. The sign was typical of signs on properties back in Venice: "Warning. Private property. Keep out."

The heat of the day bothered me more than the signage, so I climbed the chained fence and moved into the shade of a large boulder, the only structure with shade as far as the eye could see. I sat down beside the rock and picked the burrs from my socks for a long time, in a semi-meditative state. After a time I followed the high fence, once again climbed over it, and came to an old Roman road which I followed until I found a sign indicating 5 km to Logrono. I had walked some 5 km off the beaten track but, by the grace of God, in the right direction. I left Logrono at dawn after eating some wild berries and the juice, of an orange followed by some French bread stored overnight in my backpack.

Rustichello packed away quill, ink and journal and was soon on the Way again. The track from Logrono to Najera, 29.6 km, followed natural walking paths and side tracks close to main roads, passing near a man-made nature reserve and a reservoir lake. Somewhere near Navarrete, he fell into step with four Frenchmen. They exchanged the usual "Buen Camino" greetings and had wonderful conversations, ranging from education to current world economies, politics, taxes and leadership. Rustichello slowly drifted behind the Frenchmen on the remaining 10 km to Najera. Now, for some strange reason, he drifted to the past and the people who had influenced his decision to journey to Santiago. So he stopped for a brief time to rest and then began to journal; again: I was reflecting now on how some people come into our lives to teach another lesson on our spiritual journey. I remembered reading, from an unknown author, that sometimes lessons are not realised until the teacher has passed to a new way of living, or has died. You know at the time that they are meant to be there, to serve you, to teach you a lesson or to help you figure out who you are or what you want to be. All too often you never know who these people might be; they may be a friend, a neighbour, a lover, or a stranger. Your intuition knows, from the moment you lock eyes with them, that they will affect your life in some profound way. Sometimes events occur that may at first seem horrible, painful and unfair, but on reflection, you find that without overcoming these obstacles you would never have realised your full potential strength, willpower or heart.

Everything happens for a reason. Nothing happens by chance or using good or bad luck. Illness, injury, love, loss, moments of greatness or sheer stupidity – all occur to test the limits of our soul. Without these tests, whatever they may be, life would be a smooth, paved, flat road to nowhere. It would be safe and comfortable, but dull and utterly pointless. The people we meet who affect our lives and the success and downfalls we experience help us to create who we are and who we will become. Every bad experience can be learnt from; in fact, they are probably the most poignant and important ones. If someone hurts, betrays us or breaks our heart...forgive. It is the way we learn about trust and being cautious about whom we open our hearts to. If someone loves you, love them back unconditionally, because they are teaching us how to open our hearts and eyes to things. There, on The Camino Way, I resolved to make every day count, to appreciate every moment and to take from those moments everything that I possibly could. I knew that I might not experience it all again.

So, talking to people I would possibly never see again, and taking the time to listen, has been an education. I could see now that I could make of life anything I wished, I had only to act and to believe. I had created the life I had led until now, and I would create my own life in the future – but it would be a far different life than the one I had been living. I would have no regrets; now, if I loved someone, I would tell them and if I didn't like someone, I would tell them why, for communication may teach me a new way of looking at that person. I resolved to learn a new lesson in life every day. For some strange reason, at this stage of my journey, my mind kept returning to thoughts of my father and others who had died - those who influenced my life - and the lessons I had learnt by having been a part of their life on earth.

CHAPTER 5.

THE WAY, THE MYTHS AND FOLKLORE

It seems to Rustichello da Pisa that he had been re-educated to a new kind of philosophy and had a vision to focus on writing and teaching philosophy and writing books on travel and romance at some future date. The universe proved in time that this would be his lot in life as an older man in his home-town of Venice, and then once more Rustichello wrote in his journal for the King.

Leaving Logrono by the ancient pilgrim's gate Puerto del Camino, it is then back to the vineyards of La Rioja and on to this modern 12th-century town of Navarette, built by the Knights of Sepulchre, and a pause in the medieval town of Najera, with its panoramic views of the entire region. A quiet country road follows, with the La Demand Mountains to the south. Through the small decimated villages of La Rioja to the region's patron, La Virgen de Valvanera, and on to the starting point of The Monasteries Route to Yusa and Suso, monaster-ies of San Martin de la Cogoila, considered to be the birthplace of the Spanish language. Then, on to the beautiful city of San Domingo with its close history to The Camino de Santiago.

The trail from San Domingo starts on uneven terrain through wood-lands and crop fields. Near Belorando the Oca Mountains is the last range to be seen before entry to the pleasant hamlet of San Juan de Ortego, the trail reaches the mountains of Villafranca de Oca and then weaves through gorgeous woodland of oak and pine before reach-ing the town.

The Way then continues across the mountainous terrain of the Sierra de Arapuera, with views to Burgos region flats, the pilgrim descends to the river valley and the suburbs of Burgos, the home of the beauti-ful cathedral and the history of El Cid.

Thus said Rustichello in his journal for the King. It seems he had it all down to fine art now and knew how to embellish the tale much more elo-quently when face-to-face with his King so he then turned to local myth to colour his experiences:

Santa Domingo's claim to fame is the historical tale of live chickens, whose ancestors still live in the cathedral. The story goes that the German Hugonell family, father, mother and son, stayed with a farming family during their Medieval pilgrimage to Santiago. The farmer's daughter tried to seduce the son, but after he refused her she went to the authorities and accused him of theft. Upon finding silverwear items in his backpack, which had been placed there by the farm girl, he was found guilty and was hanged. The grief-stricken parents went on to complete their pilgrimage and, on their return journey, went to visit their son's hanging body. To the parents' and the authorities' surprise, the boy was still alive. The parents hurried to the magistrate and begged for their son to be cut down and forgiven. The magistrate had only just sat down to a hearty meal of fresh chicken. He replied, "He is no more alive than this roasted chicken I am about to eat".   At this, the chicken stood up and miraculously came back to life, feathers and all. In remembrance of this story, live chickens said to be descendants of the story's resurrected fowl, are kept at the cathedral. The other miracle reported was that of Saint Domingo, who cleared the road to Santiago and built bridges in the area. Legend has it that he fell asleep whilst clearing a forest, and angels picked up his scythe and continued clearing the undergrowth. I enjoyed my stay in Santa Domingo; it had quaint, neat streets with interesting shops and great food and accommodation.

Thinking about the Mass ceremony at Saint Juan de Ortega monastery, at the Mass, we adjourned to a side altar where the body of the Saint is interred, and the priest read the Pilgrim's Blessing and the Pilgrim's Prayer to St. James. It was all very moving, and a timely reminder of the purpose of my journey on The Camino, for prayers were rested: the Monastery of Saint Juan de Ortega -Pilgrim's Blessing

"Oh God, you gifted your servant Abraham of the city of Ur of the Chaldeans, safety in all his pilgrimages, and you were the guide of the Jewish people through the desert. Please, through the intercession of San Juan de Ortega, with whose tomb we are, save the children of yours who, for the love of your name walk The Camino de Santiago! I ask for them on the road companionship, guidance at the crossroads, breath in fatigue, defence in danger, shelter along the way, a gentle breeze in heat, protection before the cold light in the darkness, conso-lation in disappointment and firmness in purpose, so that with your guidance they arrive unharmed at the end of their pilgrimage and enriched thanksgiving and virtues, return them safely to their homes full of perennial joy. We ask this through Christ the Lord. AMEN."

"May the Lord, through San Juan de Ortega, direct your steps and be favourable in inseparable companionship along the way. AMEN."
"May the Holy Virgin Mary dispense her maternal protection, defend the dangers of soul and body, and under the mantle of Mother may you deserve to arrive safely at the end of your pilgrimage. AMEN"

"May San Juan de Ortega accompany you along the way and spare you from opposition and danger....and may the blessings of Almighty God, Father, Son and Holy Spirit descend upon you. AMEN" "While walking your life's path you're never alone for long on the path Santa Maria goes. Come with us to walk, Santa Maria come. Come with us for a walk. Santa Maria come."

"IN THE NAME OF JESUS, WHO IS THE WAY, THE TRUTH AND THE LIFE, GO IN PEACE AND SAN JUAN DE ORTEGA GOES WITH YOU.

I found these visits to churches, monasteries, cloisters and chapels to be welcome oases at the end of each daily journey along The Way, and a good means of escaping the heat. They were always pleasantly cool inside because of the high exposed-beam ceilings and plastered walls that were the order of the day in every holy place I ventured into. The influence of the Medieval kingdom of Narvella in The Pyrenees; The Romanesque architectural styles of the Iberian Peninsula; the Moors, who destroyed and rebuilt; and the Spanish themselves in their devotion to Saint James – all were in evidence in every historic building in northern Spain. For me, in the little chapels and churches along The Camino, all these influences were evident.

Leaving the majestic city of Burgos, its Medieval grandeur and the prome-nade on the banks of the Duero and Arlanza Rivers, Rustichello crossed the Meseta, walking among immense crop fields, through small woods of holm oak and conifers to the Medieval stronghold of Hornillos del Camino. Then, another day of walking in the peaceful vastness of the Meseta before the gradual climb up to the plateau before descending to the valley of the

River Bol and the pretty town of Castrojeriz and its 9th-century hilltop castle.

The final walk on the plain of the Burgos region leads to the highest point of the Meseta, Alto Mosterales. After crossing the Pisuera River, The Way enters the Palencia plains of Tierra de Compos, a land of fields and the Gothic architecture of its church.

The scenic route at Poblacion de Campos follows the peaceful banks of the Ucieza River to Carrion de los Condes. The natural track then proceeds along the old Roman road, with its original paved surface, which is historically used by French pilgrims on their way to Santiago. The walk then passes through many little valleys, making the route more difficult, but then emerges into peaceful oak woods and cereal fields. Here Rustichello crosses the Valderaduey River into the province of Leon, to the Medieval town of Sahagun, in the heart of the Meseta.

And so Rustichello returned to diary entries: I woke in the early morning light, to the sounds of other pilgrims in an adjoining room repacking the knapsacks for the day ahead, I washed, dressed and was on the road again as the sun came up on the horizon. The morning was again hot and dry as I entered Hontanas and found a real breakfast of orange juice, toast and coffee at the first café I came across. It had been too early and dark when I passed through San Bol to do the feet-soaking I had planned. I dispensed with the idea of taking a day off and arrived in Hontanas in broad daylight.

I had crossed the desert wasteland and reached another oasis, an ancient village of numerous springs and abundant water. I had been warned about the dangerous wild wolves that hunted in packs around the village. They were said to lay hidden in the valley of a little river so that one scarcely saw them until it was too late. Legend has it that they roamed around the village at night, attacking sheep and even humans. Because of that, in Hontanas my fellow pilgrims and I were advised that it was safest to cross the river and the desert in the middle of the day while sheep were guarded by non-ferocious dogs. I took all this with a grain of salt, as being another myth or legend, for I was beginning to muse and laugh inwardly at the folklore. I was not afraid of dogs, even wild ones.

Rustichello sat for a time under the shady of a tree when he began again to write Continuing the journey, I dismissed all fears of the dangers in nature. The possibility of encountering a wild wolf was very unlikely, and I shrugged my shoulders at the thought that nature can be both cruel and kind. I did not see a sheep in this desert country, nor any wolves, which I guessed had died out before the village' protective walls began to crumble"

He was part journalling for his later recall, so he entered the notes in his private journal. "I knew I had ample time to explore the area so, I purchased some more bandages and a jar of sweet-smelling ointment with illustrations of a Camino pilgrim and a shell brand stamped on its lid. I applied the "urgent traditional Mundi Camino" cream to my swollen ankle and blistered feet, once again dressed my wounds and put on a clean pair of socks. I assumed that the directions read something like, "traditional urgent treatment for the journey", noting that it contained petroleum jelly and Aloe Vera – with other ingredients written in Spanish which I could not understand. Tightly lacing my boots, I continued on my Camino. This routine became a daily habit and fitted in with the well-earned rest as I explored the countryside along The Way. I intended to visit.

Then he returned to writing notes for the King: Leaving the vast " Tierra de Compoa" behind, the pilgrim continues across more corn grain crop fields to reach the plateau of Leon. Along the way, the pilgrim will pass the pretty village of Reliogos and take the church of San Anton, where the remains of the 3rd-century hermit are kept. He is supposed to have cured a young girl of a disease known as St. Anthony's Fire, which caused a terrible burning sensation, loss of blood circulation and, eventually, gangrene. The 11th-century Order of St. Anthony developed a reputation for healing the disease, so, I figured that if by some miracle or past mysticism, I could be cured of my blistered feet and swollen ankle, a visit was well worth a shot. The church had long been in ruin, so my hoped-for cure had to wait until another day. In truth, all I needed was to rest my feet in cool water.

I made it to the top of the mountain, where there was a roadside stall set up with food and water for pilgrims. The enterprising Spanish trader had transported the supplies of food and water in an old wagon that was perched not far away on the other side of the mountain. Prices were not stated; there was only a simple cardboard sign with "Purchase by donation" in English on it. He probably got more money from pilgrims than he would have with fixed prices. Besides, he had a guaranteed market; after such a climb we pilgrims were definitely in need of food and water. The stall-keeper had erected umbrellas to shade pilgrims from the sun and had also provided bench seats for all to rest upon.

The climb down the other side of the mountain was just as steep as the climb up; it dropped away sharply from the 200-metre level, then up again before running level, and then easing to another 800-metre drop to the valley floor below. The dirt track had no give and my right toe felt as if a devil with a pitchfork was poking at it with every pain-filled step. I struggled, with my toes pressing to the front of my boots whenever there was a dip in the terrain. I became distracted by the enjoyment of being in the company of other pilgrims as we made our way together down the track.

A brief rest just outside the village of Castrojeriz was another necessary pause in the journey for me. I removed my boots and socks and soaked my fiery feet in a stream. A young man and his girlfriend sat down with me and copied my actions. Earlier in the day I had given him some of my magic Camino liniment which he had massaged into his feet. He said it had worked well for his swollen feet, and I had to admit that it had worked for me, too. I wondered what the Spanish ingredient was that provided the mixture's healing power; perhaps it was the presence of the ancient symbolic pilgrim on the lid with The Camino scallop shell in the background. As we sat there talking, a feather floated down from the heavens above and landed at our feet. We three looked up into the blue, but there was no bird in flight to be seen. This was typical of many strange occurrences on The Camino, and there were to be many even stranger happenings to follow down the track. Here we were, three pilgrims, total strangers, enjoying a chat with feet in the stream by the path of The Way, and nature was calling, "Birds of a feather flock together". At least that's what I was reading from the experience.

I arrived at Castrojeriz early in the afternoon and calculated that I had walked for 21 km during the day. Considering the state of my feet and the many rest stops to treat them, I thought I had done well to get as far as I had. The next day was to be a 19 km walk to Boadilla del Camino, and normally would have been an easy day for me, but with a heavy backpack still weighing me down, and foot problems, a good rest before tackling the next leg of the journey made a lot of sense. The Albergue innkeeper did the usual passport-stamping, in this case, "Casa Rural El Veredero", and I went for a hot shower, followed by two drinks and some figs and nuts at the bar. I returned to my room for a twenty-minute nap, the proprietor's mother, who was eighty in the shade, volunteered to do my washing, for which I was happy to pay the asking price.

Everywhere in the towns and villages, and to some degree in the cities, meals are today fresh and the wine and bread are usually locally produced. Spanish meal traditions are altered on The Camino, primarily to suit the pilgrims' eating habits and the opportunity to market a pilgrim meal deal in the evening. So the cena, the evening meal, becomes lunch for pilgrims on The Way, usually looking for something light to eat whilst walking the trail, and therefore preferring dinner to be the equivalent of the corrida, the Spanish lunch. The "menu peregrine", or "pilgrim's menu", is always at a low cost and is a great way to end the day and restore energy for the next day's trekking.

At this Rustichello ceased his writings for the time being even though he had many other experiences he could have written on if he chose to give it rest and would tell more on his return at the request of the King. He turned to his journal making a diary entry: I knew that I had not arrived spiritually, but I would keep on keeping on despite the difficulties, blisters and swollen ankles. It was after the steep hill at Castrojeriz that I had fallen and twisted my ankle. I was walking down a steep slope and slipped, fortunately not hitting the ground because of the support of my walking poles and boots. I'd made it to the bottom of the slope and stopped to examine the injury. I quickly massaged the area that was swelling, applied a tight bandage and continued walking despite the pain, repeating to myself, "I am strong. I can beat any pain".

Outside of San Nicolas, I came across a small pilgrims' hospital by the side of a roadside chapel, outside of which hung a Spanish flag and a sign which I translated as, "San Nicolas hospital, a peaceful chapel".

The scallop shell and the St. James' Sword of the Knights Templar were on the wall nearby. He entered the small alcove, which had been a resting place for pilgrims for decades, and took in the vista. In the historic vestibule of the chapel was a large wooden table where a nurse attended to a pilgrim, administering some tablets and water, whilst a man whom I assumed to be a doctor was tending to another pilgrim's injured hand.

Rustichello entered the foyer of a small traditional church, now serving as an emergency hospital for weak, weary and injured pilgrims, some of whom just sat on bench-like seats along a far wall appearing to be in a meditative state. He assumed they had come in to escape the heat, as it was nice and cool inside. Perhaps they were there in penance, awaiting reconciliation or baptism into a dying but traditional faith. In a corner stood a large medicine cabinet housing all types of liquid medicines, tablets, medical equipment, bandages and gloves, all of which could be seen through the glass doors and in the half-open drawers.

Guavas, a small man of Arabic appearance with shoulder-length hair, a dark beard and piercing eyes, looked at him as he busily attended to a young female pilgrim with a hand injury. He wore a full-length white robe and could have passed for an Arabic warrior if not for his small stature and skin colour. Pilgrims' bags were piled near the entry by those awaiting treatment, those merely escaping the heat and those awaiting traditional Catholic indoctrination. Guavas introduced himself while continuing to attend to the young girl's hand. He enquired about my health and I explained about my twisted ankle and blistered feet. He left the young woman and instructed me to remove the bandage and not use it again. Rustichello was rather puzzled by this, and even more so when he asked what the treatment would cost. He merely shrugged his shoulders and continued to examine his new patient's ankle and blisters. Rustichello was not aware at that time that the Spanish church picked up the tab for all medical costs, and even helped fund the local municipal Albergue on The Camino. This explained why, in the main, Albergue' worked on donations and was run by volunteers.

After cleaning Rustichello's blisters with water from a large bowl on the cabinet, he treated them with iodine and applied to stick plasters without padding directly on and over the wounds. He then led his new patient outside the building, to face the entry wall where the Spanish flag, the sword and the scallop shell hung – all reminders of what Rustichello was doing on The Camino. Guavas taught him exercises, using the wall as support, to relieve the swollen ankle and strengthen the area of the injury, and told him he would have no further problem with it and that the condition would improve on the proviso that he did the exercises every time he took a rest stop along The Way. Not content with the advice regarding his wounds and injury, Guavas also said that he was strong in body and mind and did not need to take Western medicines and that I should drink more natural juices and plenty of water, eat more natural foods such as raw vegetables, fruits and nuts. And give up coffee altogether! He placed particular emphasis on giving up anything that contained sugar and its substitutes. Rustichello upon leaving his kindly physician recalled the word of Christ "And he said unto them, Ye will surely say unto me this proverb, 'Physician, heal thyself: what so ever we heard done in Capernaum, do also in thy country." (King James Bible Luke 4:2).

A little while later he was joined by a sage of The Way who instructed him on the art of meditation:

Rustichello had many times looked for an answer to his inward soul journey. He had realised the truth of the saying: "The longest journey is the journey inward." However, with his busy life before the Camino and the subsequent troubles that befell him, the grief that he had come to accept in his state of being, the idea of meditation he never found time for in his former life, and at this moment walking with the sage he found he had much to learn from the holy man.

The sage began to instruct him with gentle words as they walked and for the first time in his life Rustichello had an inner awakening as to the mental, physical and spiritual benefit of daily meditation: His breathing slowed down, his breath became deeper and his steps slower but more deliberately conscious with each onward movement. He felt like he was floating as if he were in a zone of peaceful bliss. He was so mindful of the instruction of the sage with the smooth soft voice of reason. Rustichello was at peace and the task he had set out to do on behalf of the King, he felt more in tune with it and his surroundings.

And so listening to the sage's words as they walked he began to heed his advice "You may be sitting, or walking your Camino while observing the inhalations and exhalations of your breath. No pressure on the breathing is required; just allow your circumstances to dictate the breathing pattern.

CHAPTER 6.

LEON AND BEYOND

Thus it was that Rustichello wrote in his journal as he entered the outskirts of the city.

The "Via Traiana" trail passed more crop fields and on to the first industrial activity in approaching the route to Santiago de Compostela, The Pulcha Leonina in the Leon Cathedral is the " Sistine Chapel of Spanish architecture.

Botines and the Hospital de San Marcos add to the decor and sense of luxury. The cottages, museums, food outlets and character of the locals all evoke a vista reminiscent of a poor man's Paris.

Leon, the historic capital of the kingdom in the Middle Ages, is a historic enclave on the Camino Way

The route to the centre of Leon took him to a place such as he had never previously visited during this lifetime; he felt he was being transported back in time as he slowly wound his way through an ancient laneway past a historic wall which, Rustichello later discovered, had been built by the Romans in 29 BC when they had first established the city as a military encampment.
Then another note in his journal:

Once again, it was as if hot pokers were penetrating my toes with every step. The city's outskirts were very run-down, with slum buildings, dirty shop walls and dirty windows; ragged people were hanging about with nothing better to do than stay in the shade of alleyways,

As he came closer to the city's centre his spirits lifted and the scenery improved immensely. The first resident he encountered was a middle-aged Spanish lady who approached him and offered him a bed to stay with her. He did not know if she was offering him to be a lodger or to share her bed;

either way, he was not interested as his mind was on his mission for King Philip and his spiritual quest.

A faint expression of his mission was manifested into something new in this ancient city; a city established as a permanent settlement by the Roman military as far back as 29. BC. It was built to protect Galician gold during its transport to Rome. Rustichello was stunned by the ancient beauty of the place, so once more he journaled his notes for the king:

The sheer depth of feeling surrounding those streets engulfed me; it seemed I had walked back in time. As I walked towards the main square I was returned to the present time of modern shops, coffee houses and restaurants. I found my way to Leon's finest treasure, the sublime Gothic cathedral, with its magnificent stained-glass windows allowing the light to stream inside to steal the show. This is the fourth church to stand on this spot. Begun in 1205 restoration is still underway and I believe it will take many more years to complete. The building's serene Virgen Blanca statue welcomed me from below the central tympanum. The seats in the choir are carved with biblical characters and creative, humorous depictions of the vices, reminding me of the cheek of Michelangelo's murals on the ceiling of the chapel in Florence, visible only by climbing the steep stairs to the ceiling. The seven chapels within the Leon Cathedral contain Gothic tombs, including that of King Ordono II, with a scene from the crucifixion. In the centre of the cathedral, where Rodrigo Díaz de Viv, "the Cid," the master" is buried.

Then having explored extensively Rustichello being a weary pilgrim sought a place to lay his head. The city was alive with pilgrims like him, all exploring the side streets, which all looked daunting but exciting to visit. Rustichello made a mental note to spend an extra day there to further explore its ancient historical sites and get a feel for its beauty. He was now in a state of exhaustion, but his spirit was lifted by the sights he saw as he neared the inner sanctum. As luck would have it, he met a pilgrim who directed him to the El Burgo Ranero Albergue, the most beautiful sight for this weary traveller. This Refugio (or albergue) did not open for new pilgrims until later in the afternoon, so he contented himself with lining up with fellow pilgrims, waiting for the huge courtyard doors to open so that he could register and have his pilgrims' passport stamped.

So before he finally settled in for the night he added a few more notes to his journal. The Moors did as much restoration and building as did the Christians. In 988 the city was once again taken over by Muslims under the leadership of Al-Mansurs, who rebuilt more of the city, and it flourished as a centre of the wool industry. So I meandered my way along the cobblestone pathways and narrow streets, I was taken by the morning shadows of the buildings that spoke to me of Roman, Gothic, Muslim and Spanish peoples who had walked these ancient streets centuries before me. I somehow felt as if I was viewing the city as a reflection, like someone who gazes into a river and sees images upside-down.

He then spoke of the early history of Leon. The city was separated from the Ostrogoths in the 4th century, repeatedly invaded Roman-held territories and established great kingdoms in Gaul and Spain. They took the city of Leon by force in 586, establishing it as a centre for agriculture and, no doubt, the mining of gold. The Muslims (Moors) took the city in 712 and held it until the Spanish regained control, reconquered in 856 by..." Rustichello had fallen into a deep sleep before he finished his journal notes. He did not return there but left that to the king's discretion on his return to the French kingdom, for he could have written a full manuscript on Leon and its history but preferred to commit that to memory at another time.

Rustichello left in the early hours of the morning. On the Way again he wrote the next stage of his journey: The Camino from Leon to Ponferrada is almost level, and easy. One walks through fields of grain, corn, potatoes and apple orchards, along footpaths and dirt tracks to the prettiest village on The Camino, Hospital de Orbigo.
Here the pilgrim will cross the famous bridge 'Puente de Orbigo' with the distant scene of the Leon Mountains as the pretty hilltop city of Astorga, the capital of Margateria, is reached. The "pink" cathedral, the Gaudi lived in the C20th-inspired Episcopal Palace and the city walls are unforgettable, as are the local chocolates. Gradually, the pilgrim makes his way to the Leon Mountains and the El Bierzo region, surrounded by broom, heather and oak. The climb to Mount Irago among the broom and heather is in stark contrast with the iron cross on the mountain's top, a good point for contemplation, before descending to the lush area of El Bierzo. The mountain village of Acebo is a

peaceful place to stay, before entry into the city of Ponferrada. It was here that I, Rustichello received further instructions in the art of meditation

. You will find your own pattern and it will be natural to you alone, even if you are climbing a hill, so just be mindful of it; let all thoughts and ideas drift away. If they are important to you, they will return in some form later. Don't worry if you think you have lost the idea. I promise you won't lose it; it will come back, although perhaps in a different form. How important is it at the time, anyway? If you make this a daily practice you will feel much better able to handle life's tasks and your long walking treks will prove to be easy. Life always presents difficulties, but breathing meditative practice will help you cope, irrespective of circumstances. Don't think about this, just do the practice every day and you will view life differently."

The sage took a deep breath and continued:" Just be aware that the mind will play tricks on you, and you will find that it often wanders, particularly during early practice. Don't suffer because of this, just get back the practice of focusing on the breath. Remember, your mind has not gone anywhere, it's still there, and it's only your imagination and change occurring in the mind. In a flash, you are back with your breathing focus. You are the one who knows you are not craving anything during this mindful state of breathing. You are not trying to do anything. You just are, wherever you are in the physical world at the time, focusing on your breathing.

It was at Hospital de Orbigo, on the main street on the other side of the impressive Gothic bridge over Rio Orbigo, at the site of a Medieval jousting competition. that Rustichello was joined by an earlier companion of the road, and they crossed the historic bridge together. He had noted in his diary later:

We recalled the story of Don Suero de Quinones, a wealthy Leonese knight who had been rejected by a woman he loved; he sent out a call to knights of the Medieval kingdom, for a jousting competition to determine who was best of all the knights of the realm. The good Don locked his neck in an iron collar and swore not to remove it until he had defeated all the other knights. He defended the bridge and succeeded in his goal, freeing himself from the torment of lost love. He took the collar off and made a pilgrimage to Santiago, where he left a jewelled bracelet, which can still be seen there in the cathedral's museum. The bridge, known as "The Honorable Pass" after that event, overlooks a grove of poplars, and I imagined the display of brilliant flags standing where they now stood, trumpets blowing and the excitement of the Medieval joust!

On the other side of the bridge, Rustichello again met his little band of brothers, pilgrims off the road, and they made their way through the town and onto the track towards Astorga. He entered a note in his journal for later recall for the King: "I had walked 31.5 km that day as we crossed the zig-zag overhead pass at the entry to Astorga, now weary, but boosted with a zest for life in the company of my young friends. I resolved to shake off my lethargy and enjoyed the legendary pathway of St. James and St. Paul, who both reportedly preached in this old city. Astorga, a city of historic buildings and an awe-inspiring cathedral with an impressive Baroque façade and retablos is a very enjoyable stopover. The Celtic-influenced city was an important trading centre for the Romans, early Christians, and the Spanish; it had been destroyed by the Moors, and then rebuilt by the Christians in the mid-9th century. It flourished with the pilgrim traffic and trade, and housed many pilgrim hospitals; St. Francis of Assisi stayed in one of them during his pilgrimage in 1214. My usual end-of-day ritual, of cooling off in a beautiful place made my cathedral visit even more worthwhile.

I had fallen behind my young companions and thought that perhaps a Roland-like knight would catch up to me before I reached Foncebadon, which I hoped to do before nightfall. The Knights Templar had initially established a fort in the village, to provide refuge for pilgrims from wolves and bandits, it was influenced by both the Christians and the Muslims, and in the time of the great Charlemagne, one of his knights had married a Muslim woman from the village.

In the early evening, Rustichello made the slow, steep ascent towards Foncebadon, 4.5 km further, at the top of the mountain trail. It was still very hot when he reached a point about halfway up the mountain and realised that he had run out of water and was feeling rather parched. As luck would have it, he turned a corner on the track to find a water trough with refreshing mountain spring water running into it. He drank his fill and refilled his water flasks, soaking his feet in the chilly waters of what was possibly a drinking trough for livestock and then, after a rest, thought about camping for the night under the stars. He felt free in body, calm of mind and relaxed of spirit, with no fear of the possible consequences of sleeping out in such an isolated spot. He then entered a journal note before moving on:

However, after a short time, I thought better of it and decided to catch up with my young friends, make my way to the mountain and seek out the Monte Irago Albergue. The Roman road went through this pass, and it had been another stopover point during Roman times. However, it died as a main route after the Romans left and later became a hermitage for monks of the 10th century.

Rustichello entered the Monte Irago Albergue and encountered many pilgrims seated, waiting to share an extremely large paella in a giant pan. It had a combination of what appeared to be risotto, capsicums, onions, garlic cloves, squid, peas, and possibly parsley. He could not recognise the other ingredients, but the aroma made his mouth water as he was by now extremely hungry. The kitchen also contained the registration desk for pilgrims, but the young long-haired Spanish guy preparing the paella over the open flame chose to ignore him as he went about his business. Rustichello filled the time by looking at an old painting on a nearby wall of an Indian sage in long robes with a large crucifix adorning the walking staff held firmly in one hand. The picture was very faded, but unmistakably had been painted outside the front entrance of the albergue. It was held in a shabby wooden frame that matched the dirty walls of the small entrance, where he waited patiently until another young, greasy-haired youth in a long, dirty robe and holding a mangy-looking cat under his arm enquired about his needs. When Rustichello explained that he required a bed for the night, the greasy-headed youth waved his free arm at him and, said, "No bed left." Rustichello, said: "I am the Master of the Arts, on a mission for the King of France.", "Awww! Senor, you have a bed!" Rustichello made his way to the back of the Albergue, dodging sheep, goats, chickens and a mule. The Albergue accommodation adjoined the animals' stalls and the chicken coop, and he got the last of a horse hair mattress and proceeded to dump his gear on the floor before making his way back to the kitchen to join the rest of the pilgrims for a meal. He returned to the mattress to lay out his sleeping gear for the night and was surprised to find his Italian walking companions, whom he had met during the twilight hours in the village of Rabanal in the valley below, on the mattresses next to him. They had decided to venture up the mountain for the night after all.

The Pilgrims all left the Monte Irago Albergue after a complimentary breakfast of bread, jams and fruit. The sun had not yet appeared and the morning was cool and full of silence; no sound of crowing roosters, of sheep, goats or mules and not a sound of wild dogs. This surprised Rustichello a little, as he had heard so many mystical stories of encounters with vicious dogs around Foncebadón but maybe it was the time of day when the animals, and the dogs, were enjoying the peace and cool before the heat of the day set in again. He stopped at a marker to write more in his diary for the King;

We passed horse pastures and the ruins of Guacelmo's Medieval pilgrim hospital, ascending through scrubby heather and gorse to arrive at the highlight of every pilgrim's journey on The Camino, the Cruz Ferro. The Cruz Ferro, almost the highest point of the entire Camino Frances, consists of a tall wooden pole topped by an iron cross. This ancient Celtic monument was first erected by the Romans in dedication to their god, Mercury, the protector of travellers. It was later crowned by the cross and renamed a Christian site in the 9th century by the hermit, Guacelmo. For centuries, pilgrims have brought a stone, or some icon of personal significance representing their burden, to this place; and those from foreign lands bring something from their homeland. The stone, or the item representing the burden, is left here, leaving the pilgrim lighter both literally and figuratively for the journey ahead, The decaying rocks now form a small hill at the foot of the pole, although why pilgrims now pray, let go of their burdens and pay homage here to whatever it is that attracts them to such a desolate place is beyond comprehension. I watched as many pilgrims climbed the mound of rock at the foot of the pole, standing in silence while letting go of their burdens. Some cried silently, wiping their eyes; others, like me just stood, watching, in a kind of vacuum of nothingness.

Another journal note: *Our journey's pathway passed the little Refugio de Manjarin, hosted by Thomas, who considered himself a Knight Templar, the last of the Knights, serving drinks and snacks to passing pilgrims. The rustic appeal of Thomas' humble abode, with no running water, made our brief stop another memorable experience. The rough signs on the verandah of this strange Spanish Knight's abode detailed the distances to Santiago and other cities on The Camino. We walked through fields of heather, arriving at a wide path up to a large cairn for a breathtaking view of Ponferrada in the valley floor below. We then commenced our sharp descent for the next 3.9 km to El Acebo. Once more, we had lost the seriousness in our nature and, falling into step along The Camino, began to tell stories and jokes to each other as the sun beat down on us, once more ignoring our discomfort, inner pain or aspirations, just living in the moment.*

Rustichello's next diary entry was for the King on his progression of the Camino.

Ponferrada to Sarria .Memories of the impressive Templar Castle in Ponferrada fade as the pilgrim walks through the lush pastures of the El Birzo, nestled in the mountains. Flavours of exquisite cured meats and delicious cherries from the local villages and a visit to the garden of Iglesia de Santiago at Villafranca, and Puerta del Pardon (the "Forgiveness Gate") all nourish the body and the heart. The Way follows the valley via the Valcarca River before a challenging ascent to the ranges of Os Ancares and Sierra do Courel, passing through the Ranadoiro Mountains and across the Alto do Polo, descending

CHAPTER 7

THE FINAL LEG OF THE CAMINO

Into the village of Triacastela strode Rustichello where he stopped to record more into his journal.

The San Xil Camino offers scenery that fortifies the pilgrim's spirit, whilst the optional narrow forest track slices through typical Galician oak woods; an alternate route to Sarria, through Samos, with its impressive monastery. This is perhaps the first town in the region where the pilgrim can enjoy the delicacy of freshly cooked octopus. Walking across the valley to the river and following the path of the river to Sarria is a wonderful acknowledgment that man cannot duplicate that which nature provides.

The Celtic settlement of Ponferrada. The city had been a Roman mining town, later destroyed by the Germanic invaders and the Visigoths before being rebuilt by the Romans. It was again destroyed by the Muslims (Moors) and recaptured and again rebuilt by the Spanish.

We entered the city over the pilgrim bridge, built originally by the Romans but unusually reinforced by steel beams zig-zagging above the modern walkway. The city's modern name, Ponferrada, derives from the Latin, Pons Ferrata, meaning Iron Bridge. Ponferrada had been a booming pilgrimage town, with a diversity of merchants, including Franks and Jews who were protected back then as the town rejected the call for segregated communities.

We made our way to the historic Templar Castle on the town's outskirts. The Knights Templar's duties were, traditionally, to protect pilgrims and give them refuge. We went across the drawbridge and through the main gateway, with its impressive Templar coat-of-arms above the door. Although fascinated to be walking in the halls of the brave knights of old and viewing the relics on display, we were unable to see more of the historic parts of the castle, Those areas were closed to visitors, and are reported to hold all kinds of secret Templar symbols – particularly inside the twelve towers, which represent the twelve months of the year and the twelve disciples of Christ.

Rustichello with his newfound pilgrim companions left the urban area of Ponferrada and followed the trail into the scenic green of the vineyards, cherry orchards and wildflowers towards the mountains of Galicia and the beautiful Villafranca del Bierzo, among the foothills of the Rio Burbia. We had covered a distance of 27.1 km, in high temperatures, to Ponferrada, and then headed on towards Villafranca, another 24.7 km north. The 16.7 km to Cacabelos, which had been the administrative centre for the Romans' gold mining, was the goal for the day. On the outskirts of town, we viewed an old mill and a wooden olive press as a landmark with directions there en route to the Albergue.

Rustichello was weary from lack of sleep, as the albergue in Sarria had housed seventy small bunks, and the after-effects of waking in pain, coupled with being woken many more times by snoring and movement from fellow pilgrims had not helped matters.

It had been good to start walking early, after a quick breakfast. He had wandered off the beaten track the day before and gone quite a few kilometres in the wrong direction and was now determined to focus on the yellow arrow markers and plod on alone. Sarria is famous for its antique fairs, but as none had been scheduled for that week, and as the reconstructed tower of a Medieval castle held no attraction, he had decided to keep walking. Although having already jettisoned 2 kilos of his overweighted backpack a week earlier, Rustichello calculated that his backpack still weighed around 13 kilos and, still thinking about the excess weight he had carried for the better part of 700 km, he resolved to send forward by coach at least 3 kg to Santiago when he reached the next larger village with a trading post.

The blisters had all but healed, but his feet were hot and swollen from the constant pounding and the effects of an extremely hot summer's day. Many lessons this pilgrim of The Way had learnt about long-distance walking while on the Camino.; to wear only cool clothing in the heat; drink plenty of fluid; keep energy levels up with healthy food; wear sandals whenever possible; carry no more than 10% of one's body weight. He made a mental note to write this information in his journal for future reference. of his quest.

Ever mindful of his quest.on behalf of the King and the burden of his sin, he had come to believe he also learnt a lot about his defects of character.

The former merchant and 'Master of the Arts' kept himself content by singing songs, composing poems, stopping frequently to cool his feet and updating his journal. He had crossed the Medieval Ponte Aspera Bridge and the River Celerio when leaving Sarria then climbed the peak to Alto de Paramo, which had been difficult in the heat. Then came the trek through an oak forest to the hamlet of Vilei and on to Barbados, a distance of 6 km which had been slower going. The days of Barbadelo being a thriving commercial centre were mentioned in the Codex Callixtinus, that 11th-century manuscript attributed to Pope Callixtinus II, that he had carried with him, as a gift from King Philip to help him on his Camino. He had packed only a small snack and supplemented it with a gourd of water which he filled at a nearby fountain. The snack, mixed nuts and some cake were all adequate to see him through until the evening meal.

Reenergised, Rustichello walked a further 12.7 km on a gradual downward slope, regularly passing small abandoned hamlets and several small towns before arriving at Mercadoiro, another desert oasis. He had walked 16.9 km that day and now had the fire in his belly to push on to Santiago. Passing the marker indicating the final 100 km to Santiago, and recalling the rocks, notes and pictures that lay in a pile near the marker on a stone fence nearby, a sign had been erected, reading, "Lay down your sorrow". This was a monument for those who had not walked the entire Way and let go of their burdens at Cruz Ferro, near Foncebadon. Many pilgrims were content to walk only the final 100 km to Santiago and have their passports stamped at places of rest, and churches along The Way, walking only that distance to qualify for their Compostela certificate at Santiago!

Rustichello awoke early the next morning and was soon on The Way. The road dipped down for the 3 km to Vilacha, passing the only albergue there, a restored building draped with flags from around the world. As it was too early in the morning for the café bar to be open, he pushed on. Soon, Portomarin could be seen across the river, so he made a detour across the long bridge over the Rio Mino and climbed the stairway into the village. The climb up the steep stairs to the small village was worth the effort. The old stone buildings of the historic part of the town were removed, stone by stone, and a modern township had been erected high on a hill near the river. He took out his journal on arrival and made a note for his king:

The bridge I had crossed to reach Portomarín over the Río Miño had been rebuilt many times; it was wide-spanned, crossing the river at a strategic point from which ruins of the ancient Roman city could be seen during low tide. Al-Mansur destroyed an early bridge during his campaign of devastation in 997. It was later rebuilt by the Spanish but again destroyed during the war between Queen Urraca and her husband. She had the bridge rebuilt, along with the pilgrim hospital. The Church recognized that the bridge needed protection, and the role fell to The Order of Santiago, and later to The Order of San Juan de Jerusalem. It's great that the bridge still stands, as it was a wonderful feeling in the early morning to cross the bridge, climb the steep stairs and enter the town of Portomarín.

Rustichello walked the next 8 km slowly in the heat, climbing a gradual slope to the tiny hamlet of Gonzar, walking beside some impressive oak trees, then he wrote again in his journal for the King: "... on a dirt path to Castromajor, resting from the heat there in a Romanesque church where a wooden statue of a virgin stands. A traditional legend recounts that a basket of pig snouts was left as a sacrifice at the church during the time the Moors controlled the area. When the offeror returned the next day, the snouts had turned into coal. Amazed, the Christian pocketed one of the lumps and later found that it had turned into gold. She hurried back to the church to find the basket empty. The locals could not tell me what the lesson of the story was.

Rustiochello had walked 25 km in extreme heat, and whilst the route was mainly across rolling hills, nothing had been steep and, all in all, it was an enjoyable day in the country. He reached Portos in the cool of the evening and stayed in its only, small, albergue. Knowing he had a long, 28.4 km journey the next day, he had the evening meal early and set off for bed for a good night's sleep. He was more motivated now in reaching Santiago and resolved to content himself with conversations along The Way with fellow pilgrims instead of becoming distracted by historical monuments. Leaving his little bunkhouse in the darkness, he decided to try an experiment and walk by instinct in the dark. It was only early morning and sunrise would not be for at least an hour. It was pleasant in the cool of the early morning, catching what little breeze there was before sunrise, and wishing it would rain a little to soften the blow of the heat that each day provided. He was walking in relatively cool conditions and was grateful for that.

Rustichello had left his companions and walked on alone when he come upon a most unusual albergue. There he journaled once again for his King. The walled entry to his ranch-style abode had a most curious folk-art painting of young Jesus playing cards with San Antonio de Padua. The famous Saint from Portugal, born in Lisbon in 1195 and educated into The Order of St. Augustine, spent eight years in the convent in Portugal to which the relics of five Franciscan martyrs had been brought from Morocco. These relics inspired him to follow in the footsteps of those heroes of the faith and, after extreme opposition from his Order, he finally obtained consent to join the Franciscans. He was granted permission to go to Africa to preach to the Moors, but after severe illness at sea, he returned to Assisi where a chapter of the Order was in progress.

He was ignored by the Order and remained in obscurity, but providence revealed to the Franciscans what a treasure they had acquired, and San Antonio (St. Anthony) was made professor of theology and successfully taught this subject at Bologna, Toulouse, Montpellier and Padua. He later gave up teaching to work as a preacher and as an accomplished orator, travelling through France, Spain and Italy. He was regarded as a legendary hero even in his own lifetime, and many miracles were attributed to him.

As a child, I was taught of St. Anthony's miracles, and to pray for his intercession if I'd lost something. Strange as it seemed to me on my Camino, I recalled that the many times I had prayed about a missing item, he always managed to find it and return it to me. Throughout my adult life, despite giving up my traditional Catholic religion, I never forgot St. Anthony and, to this day, still ask him for help when something goes amiss; he has never let me down, although it may just be a coincidence, or a superstition on my part. I prefer to think not, but I did wonder, on my entry to that ranch-style albergue, what on earth was symbolized by the picture of St. Anthony playing cards with Jesus, on a wall in a remote village on The Camino.

Rustichello was thinking over the previous 700 km and of the people he had met during the pilgrimage. The meeting with the young German backpacker when we ran out of water and found a well in The Pyrenees; enjoying the company of the Irish mother and daughter and their stories of the land of their forefathers; the spirituality of the two young Canadian women, the Danish artist and his actor son; laughing with the Dutch kids; singing with the Belgians; listening to the beautiful singing of the South African brothers and sisters; being poetic with the young Germans and his band of brothers; eating with the Greeks and Italians; passing time with the French and the two Spanish beauties; influenced by the English teacher's freedom and the determination of the retired German ballet teacher; appreciating the kindness of an albergue volunteer and the charity and goodwill of the North and South Americans. There seemed to be so many other pilgrims to be grateful to, and all crossed his mind.

Whilst it became laborious, he made another note to his King: Yes, The Camino is truly a step back in time and a letting go of burdens, but it was also the experience – more often than not for me of being influenced and impressed by the people I met along The Way. My journey was drawing to a close and I trusted that I would get to meet many more people, hear their stories, share their joys and lend an ear to their pain and suffering as had been done by others for me. My inner discernment had already been expressed in the outward signs and experiences I had and would continue to as I wound my way to Santiago.

As he walked through the green vista of vineyards, cherry orchards and fields of wildflowers, the mountains of Galicia loomed before him. It was but a short trail of about 8 km to the Villafranca del Bierzo where the final and most beautiful town of The Camino would be a brief oasis and rest stop before treading the happy path of destiny once more. A well-earned rest stop before setting out to complete the next stage of the journey to La Faba, some 34 km further. The pathway from his overnight albergue climbed steadily for the next 32 km, and he calculated that his plan to stay in Villafranca del Bierzo should take no longer than an hour if he was to make it to La Faba at a reasonable pace that day.

My walking was now in this zone of awareness; my feet doing the walking while my body and mind did nothing but stay on course for the ride. I was mastering feelings and emotions, intent on kindness to myself and compassion for other pilgrims on The Way. Outside my zone, my feet ached and my body was wracked with the pain of the strain of what now seemed a never-ending journey. Just for now, my soul loved and my ego was in check, content to merely roll with the ever-constant drumming of my feet. It is said that the brain knows three steps ahead of where your feet will land. In my current state of mindfulness, the brain was in neutral, the body relaxed and the feet were in charge.

The pilgrim noted all this in his journal, for Rustichello was intuitive of the ability to connect with a power greater than beyond mind and senses, and now sensitive to the flow of energy coming to him from beyond, driving his body onward despite the burden of his backpack and the bag of gold for the King's sin. The connection was deeper now; the flow of energy seemed to be coming from nature and the universe surrounding him. The connection flowed to fellow pilgrims, this place and this moment in time. He was no longer a beast of burden with a heavy backpack; he seemed lighter and his mind was open to guidance.

He was now connected to a nature of divine oneness and a consciousness of higher awareness. The thought of poems he had written on his journey once again entered his head and, for a moment he was guided by the intention to write it all as a book. He just as quickly dismissed this idea as he did not want to lose the flow of energy that had come over him. The thought of writing a book was, in his limited belief, developed through fear and a need to express inner feelings. It was not something to publish for the world to see, he thought. At the time, he was not attuned to the fact that he would write many books, including poetry and write songs about the Camino. He buried the thought as his feet continued to march to the beat of a different drummer. However, the seed had been planted, and it was that seed that would evolve into his future mission after he completed the Camino de Santiago and his duty to the King.

He had written once again in his journal for the King: "I had heard it said that some people receive intuitive guidance from ascended masters; others access it through daily automatic writing, dreams or past-life regression. Whatever the technique, this day I was open to the lessons that applied to me at that time: the handing over to a power greater than me, a pathway to a higher being. It surprised me. I did not do this more often allowing my brain to do the hard yards. The brain's manner of treading life's path had led me to depression and misery. Here and now I had found a new way; I had now come to believe that it was always the way. The choices I had made in my life had been driven by fear and the need to control; now there was a different pathway."

"My task now was to transcend my limits and those of my greater consciousness. I had an inner warning of the dangers of illumination. It was now a time to let go of all that the world had taught me and to focus on training my mind and body to be open and conscious of higher awareness, otherwise, the power to transform would be blocked. It was coming to me now that this higher consciousness was a gift, and in that state of being, I needed less and would not ever be afraid again. It was a means of expressing love in a blissful state of generosity of the spirit. I would do what I love to do best, share myself with life and with other people. The need to be connected to this higher awareness would require openness to learning; to be open to what is, not to the ways of the world any longer, but to the ways of the spirit, my spirit."

The sense of the higher awareness had left Rustichello and he had walked a long distance without actually being conscious of it. His belief had been tested and had come up wanting. He resolved then and there from this experience to continue to test his beliefs. In the cool of this Spanish morning, the spirit had revealed to him the vital need to evolve to higher awareness. His logical mind told him that he still needed to be in this world but not of it; to do the things he had to do, but to hand over to this inner awareness, this higher power; to be truly alive; to have faith; to be strong and spiritually powerful. It was the lesson of The Camino. Doing all this would be his future quest over and above his duty to his King.

Rustichello once again felt the burden of his backpack and the constant pain in his feet and returned to notes in his journal for, later recalling: He was on his road less travelled on this Camino to Santiago. Thousands of travellers had walked this pilgrimage before him, and no doubt many would do so in the future. This was a time for reflection and introspection; unexplained happenings; logic giving way to myth and In the clear daylight of this plodding journey, towards the end of his Camino, he wrote: I resolved to not go there now but rather to focus on the steps of my travel on this hot Spanish morning. My thoughts somehow drifted to who I was and what I am now all about; the mindful image that I had logically determined and sought to have some outward symbol of, had seemed to be a worthy quest to fulfil on my journey. It was to be the outward fulfilment of a myth at the end of the rainbow at Santiago which, through accomplishing my inner mission, would result in me completing and producing a result that would be worthy of my cause and that of the king. It was proving to be another myth, buried upon yet another myth. The inner movement of my thoughts, emotions, feelings and desires were, in fact, more of a mindfulness of sharp spiritual perception and judgment. My becoming sensitive to my ever-changing movements and understandings were questions that came from I knew not where, they were leading me in a spiritual sense.

Then he began to write of part of the spiritual journey he had overlooked but thought worth journaling for King Philip: In my head I heard, "Trust in the slow work of God", but I was still in the darkness of my way, stumbling like a blind man towards some unknown light, perhaps to some new enlightenment. I began to hand it all over and felt as if I were being asked to walk a tightrope without a safety net. Maybe this was so, and the spirit within me, which I was beginning to understand runs the show, was taking me from my head to my heart, and was taking hold. So my pace slowed as I made each painful step on what seemed a treadmill of repetition. I began to recall that a sign I had been given many times in the past, and which I had chosen to ignore, was the real purpose of doing my Camino de Santiago. I had thought that it was all about letting go of past burdens, and seeing if I still had any affinity with the religion of my childhood. I had set out to discover whether my vision of love would manifest itself on The Camino Way and to get in touch with an outward symbol of my inner self that I would carry forth like some knight of old in a modern world. The Way had, for me, become all those things and more, for it was leading me down a pathway from a well of darkness where the dragon of my fear existed and from where, in time, a lotus flower of creative ideas and actions would spring. The strange happenings of my Camino were not yet over, but for the time being, I put aside all thoughts of strange events, miracles, historic churches and the reasons for my journey as, with every step I now focused only on the determination to complete this journey of discovery.

Then he wrote of the Camino shell as it related to himself on the journey. The pilgrim's shell and the sword symbol of St. James of Santiago that many pilgrims wore to indicate that they were on the pilgrimage were not my symbols, but those of all who had walked the many routes to Santiago from past times until this day. So many pilgrims wore this shell, symbolizing that they were walking to Santiago either for their inner journey of discovery or merely to take a long walk, meet new people and enjoy The Way. I chose to not wear the shell identifying myself as a pilgrim; this weary, dust-laden merchant with his heavy backpack is on a mission for his king for the forgiveness of sin. A symbol of the traditional pilgrim who walked for penance, pardons and meditative enlightenment in the past.

Rustichello now entering Galicia, the last of the autonomous regions of The Camino and home of the much anticipated Santiago de Compostela. The official language of Galicia is Spanish, but more than 90% of the population speaks the Galician dialect. he wrote once more in his journal. "While excavations have shown evidence of megalithic prehistoric culture in Galicia, the region was later settled by Celtic tribes who later became known as Galicians. Much of the Celtic culture remains, even the bagpipe music, which we would experience along The Way and at our destination. The people, although friendly, displayed the Celtic nature of fierce independence, much like the Scots. and similar to what those of Basque background had displayed during my time in The Pyrenees. In this inward and outward journey of spirit,

The final path to the city passes through eucalyptus forests and several small villages before reaching Monte de Gozo, from where the first glimpse can be had of the Santiago Cathedral's spires. The last 5 km into the city can often involve an atmosphere of jubilant pilgrims, singing and shouting their congratulations to others who have completed the Camino journey.
So it was that Rustichello continued his final journal entries: of his Camino:

"The atmosphere continues in the Plaza de Obradoiro, the large plaza facing the western façade of the cathedral, where pilgrims gather now as they did in the past times; there to meet once again, having come so far to reach their common objective, the Cathedral de Santiago. There they congregate by the hundreds, in time for the Pilgrims' Mass and to witness the "smoke belcher", the 'botafumeiro', the world's largest censer for spreading incense smoke. This ceremony is repeated daily, at noon, as it has always been historically. After the Mass, pilgrims visit the burial place of St. James, behind the main altars and touch the golden statue of Santiago. It is there that I, Rustichello, lay down the bag of gold for the sin of my King, and then for proof of my Way, The final tradition, I obtained the Compostela Certificate for having completed the journey.

Historical evidence suggests that Santiago was once a Roman city, followed by Visigothic rule. Many stories of spiritual happenings, ghosts and witches accompany the myths in my mind; thoughts of the presence of the body of St. James; of the Knights Templar protecting The Way for Medieval pilgrims; the myth of St. James manifested to led the Spanish army in battle to drive the Moors from the lands of Galicia. Still, my Catholic upbringing steeled me to celebrate the church ritual and pay homage to the Saint, irrespective of my personal opinions. It was, after all, written in the old Codex Calixtinus Compostela:

"The most excellent city of the Apostle, complete with all delights, having in its care the valuable body of St. James, on account of

He continued to write in his journal The Camino takes the pilgrim through pretty villages and peaceful hamlets under the shade of many old oak trees on quiet country roads. The Way passes the beautiful Romanesque church in the village of Barbadelo before crossing the River Miño and a rise uphill to Serra de Ligonde.The pilgrim passes the hamlets of Gonzar and Ventas de Narón, the Romanesque churches of Santa María in Castromajor and Eirex, where a statue of Daniel with the animals, and one a pilgrim, are featured. The trail continues downhill, past the village of Casanova, steeped in myth, and on to the village of Leboriero and the lively markets of Melide for local octopus, the most classic dish of Galicia.

The Camino crosses several streams and follows a forest track to the village of Boente and its church of Santiago. The Medieval village of Ribadisco and the town of Arzua, with their churches of Santa María and Magdalena, are a fitting way to prepare for the final leg to Santiago.The remaining pathway to Santiago takes the pilgrim through woods, sleepy villages and across streams

Lavacolla, on the outskirts of Santiago, is where pilgrims wash in the river in preparation for their arrival in Santiago. Rows of eucalyptus trees line the way to Monte de Gozo, where the pilgrim catches the first glimpse of the Cathedral of Santiago. It is traditional to attend the Pilgrim's Mass at the cathedral while delighting in the stark architecture and the spiritual and cultural "Mecca" of Santiago. Entering the township of Villafranca del Bierzo, I was struck by the beauty of this Medieval town with its Renaissance touch, despite the blemish on the landscape of modern buildings. I had entered the main gateway, past the Iglesia de Santiago, with its doorway for pilgrims who were too sick to walk to the main entrance – considered to be the essential way to enter if you hoped to gain indulgences from the church. This holy place of worship and recovery was, according to legend, built by Saint Francis of Assisi himself on his pilgrimages, for he had achieved so much during his brief time in Spain.

CHAPTER 8.

MISSION ACCOMPLISHED

Rustichello had laid down so many burdens while walking the traditional way so many pilgrims had done before this journey for the King of France, and he needed to lay down one more in his quest not just for the King but for himself.

I was searching for the fulfilment of the myth, the sword of St. James the disciple of Christ, who probably never walked on Spanish soil, never mounted a white steed and never led a great military charge against the Moors. The historical facts disproved the myth, but the myth remains, and many other pilgrims throughout the centuries have been attracted to the story and ventured on the pathway to Santiago; pilgrims in search of their own heart's desire, laying down burdens, letting go, healing, in companionship, in a spiritual quest or just to do the long walk. Fact or fiction, the story of St. James remains and the journey itself is real for every pilgrim who takes to the road and lets their feet do the walking.

And so it was that Rustichello by the last day of the sixth week of his allotted time was able to return to the King and stood before him to report on his assignments and told of his mission and what had been accomplished. Rustichello then recounted to King Phillip how it was that he had walked the Camino while doing the King's duty in fulfilling his mission for him. He handed over his journal for the King to observe the details of his journey of The Way. He told the King of the presence of Moor troops, where he had cited them and how he had completed two of his assigned duties. He also handed over his certificate of completion of the Compostela as further proof.

Then he lay before the King, to his great surprise, wrapped in a cloth of fine silk the sword of so many myths, Durandal, the sword of of Roland. As he then related " It was on his return journey via the Roncesvalles Pass that I, Rustichello was to remove the Roland sword Durandal from the rock in which it had been embedded some 11 centuries earlier and deliver it to you, King Philip as I had agreed to do in your mission for me. On arrival at Roncesvalles, I found a place to lay my weary head in the monastery dormitory for monks. I was then invited to supper with the monks and it was over a meal that I was given the key to what had happened to Durendal before it was finally embedded in the rock face not thirty minutes walk from where the holy men then sat. I, Rustichello had asked the goodly friars for their version of events as to what transpired in the battle when Roland died."

Rustichello continued: "It was the elder of the priest who suggested I go and search their archives at the basement of the monastery for documents written by two knights of the time, one having been recorded there by Sir Fermin who had been given charge over Roland's sword Durendal to use as a banner in leading the charge of Charlemagne in the final battle against the forces of evil of the Moors lead by Baligant, the Emir, the heathen who was given charge over the lands by the dying king Marsil of Spain. And Sir Lancelot, another of Cheramanger's noble knights was granted the privilege of having the horn Oliphant to carry as his banner into battle ."

So he told King Philip that it was he, Rustichello, who then hurried to the archives room and uncovered the two documents in question, and to his great surprise he soon learnt how the use of the Durendal Sword and horn had been used in the final battle against the Moors well after Roland's death and yet the sword was still embedded in the rock face nearby as was Roland's dying wish hereafter.

"Sir Fermin retold the story of Roland and the fact that the sword had been recovered with the horn under the dead body of Roland, for at the time none of Charlemagne's knights was aware of Roland's failed attempt to embed the sword in the rock, for he hid it from his enemy under his own body before he took his last breath. The sun didn't darken then nor did the earth tremble, but it did for Sir Fermin and Sir Lancelot when they arrived at the location where Roland had died. At that time they had built a rock cairn to commemorate the place of Roland's death and housed within it the 'Oliphant' horn. Whilst they were busy building the pile of rocks to house Roland's horn, the sun darkened, the earth trembled and a crack appeared in the cliff rock face nearby. Sir Fermin had then quickly driven Durendal deep within the crack that had appeared and no sooner had he done so than the Rock face moved again sealing the sword deep within the rocks and rendering it irremovable. Sir Lancelot had likewise written a similar document but added that they had to rebuild the cairn a second time after the earthquake. I, Rustichello noticed that the knights had countersigned both documents as witnesses to each other proof of the validity of their story.

And so it was that Rustichello related how he had arrived at the place of the sword where Roland had breathed his last, and had knelt at the cairn in reverence. Whilst he was doing so a storm brewed and the earth moved as if in a quake and the Durendal sword came loose from its-sealed state. In bowing to King Philip he presented the sword with both hands raised. and said: "Thus it was I was able to remove the sword from its former trap in the rock without so much as any effort at all."

King Philip was amazed and at the same time was taken aback, for he had no way of holding Rustichello after the allotted time of three months as his temporary replacement on his throne. He had therefore to devise another plan to hold him a little longer for he now knew of the gathering of Moor troops in Spain as a consequence of Rustichello's report, and he knew he would need this Master of the Arts in his charge for the foreseeable future until he felt his kingdom secured from invaders.

Then it was that the discerning Rustichello, through intuition had realised that King Philip was in further need of his services beyond the terms of their mutual agreement. The King therefore was taken aback again by Rustichello's next comment: " My king, as you can see the Durendal sword is in good shape. I have taken the liberty to clean it and have it polished to its former appearance. when Emperor Charlemagne first gave it to Roland. I would be very grateful therefore if you extended my service to you to lead any charge you wish of me after the appointed three months, but with one proviso, that if my former employers, the Polo brothers should return in the meantime I will be released from any further duty to you."

"Rustichello," said the King: " I will be honoured to do so, and because you have completed the task I assigned you; you can now take over my throne." The king stepped down and embraced his brave knight with a kiss on each cheek. " Furthermore," said the king: " Here are the monies in advance in the form of gold nuggets for you to clear your debts to the Jewish banker in Venice, thus gaining credibility with him, just in case you be need of his services in the future"

So it was that Rustichello, after serving his three months on the throne in the absence of King Philip was then assigned as war leader to overthrow the Moor's strongholds throughout the kingdom of Spain. As it happened he crisscrossed northern Spain and won many battles against Moorish troops and strongholds but despite his best efforts and his use of Durendal, the singing sword of Roland, he could not remove them from their stronghold of the Iberian Peninsula. It would take another two centuries before Spain would be rid of the Moors and Christendom would reign again.

Meanwhile, the young seventeen-year-old Marco Polo who had just graduated with high distinctions in Greek and Latin languages was keen to establish his credentials in his father and uncle's business as a merchant in Venice before their return. He had got word from a ship's captain that they had made some progress along the Silk Road into Mongolia and had an audition with Kublai Khan, the Khan of Khan. There had been a civil war at the time in the Mongolian Empire but circumstances beyond that were not known by the ship captain's messenger. Marco had been advised that the Polo brothers were safely on board a ship bound for Venice and that they would arrive within three months. Marco therefore was in great need of his friend and sponsor as a licensed merchant of Venice.

Marco made it his business to know and become aware of Rustichello's employment circumstances with King Philip 111 of France and his former debt to the local Jewish banker. It was his intelligence and cunning that forced him to find out all that related to the business and the merchant.

Rustichello, who had been left in charge of the business in the Polos brothers's absence was teaching him the merchant trade when tragedy had struck. So Marco set to work reconnecting with all the customers who had purchased merchandise through the family business, whilst formerly under Rustichello's management, telling them of the fact that the Polo brothers would return within the specified time and that his friend and sponsor in the business, Rustichello would soon return to take charge. He then went to the effort of writing to the suppliers in Porto, Portugal where Rustichello had obtained his last shipment. Then he arranged with a coachman to deliver to Rustichello via the King's palace in Paris what he had done and that he was in great need of his return to service in Venice, with particular emphases on the return of the Polo brothers.

So it was that Rustichello was released from his duties to King Philip 111 of France and headed for Porto, Portugal to obtain products for shipment to customers in England. He sent a letter praising Marco for his efforts in making his task much easier and would arrive back in Venice one month before the Polo brothers and there he would teach young Marco all that he knew so that he too would prove to be a great merchant of Venice like his father and uncle had proven to be.

True to his word Rustichello arrived back in Venice one month before the Polo brothers arrived from the Arabian desert and beyond the Far East frontiers where they had been trading extensively The faithful employee of the Polo brothers arrived with a caravan of supplies of dried fruits from the Algarve (figs, grapes, and almonds) salt from Setúbal and Aveiro all sources from his Porto connections which would prove to be a profitable export to northern Flanders and England, through the Venice port of call.
Rustichello, whilst in Porto, the main export link for Port wine, arranged for the packaging, transport, and export of the fortified wine to clients in England. The shipment was loaded onto a three-mask caravelle-like small ship, the safest means of transport then. The cargo was on the high seas destined for the Polo brothers' English clients by the time Rustichello and his young charge Marco Polo had unpacked the caravan of the supplies in the Polo's Venice warehouse.

Rustichello had returned with a clean slate to the Jewish money lender in Venice and having cleared all his debts reestablished his ownership of the land, family home, horses and stables. In addition, he purchased a small Caravelle ship and employed a sea captain and crew to carry cargo for him to England as a separate business from his employment with the Polo merchants of Venice. He intended to make a further deal with the Polos that he would continue to be their employee in the ordering and delivery of produce to their warehouse from Porto, Portugal and abroad, giving priority to them but only on the basis that they sold him at cost one-third of all purchases arranged on their behalf. He would further offer his services to oversee the loading of their cargo destined for foreign lands as well as his supplies and would act as their agent in London when their ships arrived there. The astute merchant realised that the Polo brothers would be in greater need of his services should they wish to return to the Far East and trade on the Silk Road bringing back even more unheard-of produce from those foreign lands.

As to Marco Polo, he was now the sixteen-year-old son of Niccolò Polo, who by a twist of fate had been left in his charge. Well, Rustichello knew that the young man was capable of becoming a great merchant himself should the Polo brothers not take up, Rustichello's offer.

Rustichello whilst waiting for the return of his employers was recalling how he came to take charge of the boy. He was thinking back to sixteen years earlier in 1254 when father Niccolo and uncle Maffeo sat off as merchants to trade on the Silk Road. Little Marco's father left for Asia before the child was born, and would return when the boy was a teenager. He may not even have realized that his wife was pregnant when he left.

So when the elder Polos returned to Venice they found that Niccolo's wife had died and left behind a 16-year-old son named Marco. The boy must have been surprised to learn that he was not an orphan. Two years later, the teenager, his father, and his uncle would embark eastward on another great journey. In the meantime, to Niccolo Polo's relief, his cousins had provided Marco with food, clothing and shelter, and under the guidance of Rustichello, he had completed secondary education and received distinctions in mathematics and the sciences, and in particular became highly skilled as a linguist in French, Latin and Greek. The use of languages would become his stock in trade, especially in diplomatic relations with the Mongol emperor, the Khan of Khans. Marco in his later travels furthered his language skills, his fluency flourished in Arabic languages and Mongol dialect and the common root language used by that great Mongolian Khan, a Turkic language spoken by his offspring and Mongolians, particularly in diplomatic relations.

Thanks to these enterprising merchants Venice flourished as the major trading hub for imports from the fabulous oasis cities of Central Asia, India, and far-off wondrous Cathay (China). Except for India, the whole expanse of Silk Road Asia was under the control of the Mongol Empire at this time. Genghis Khan had died, but his grandson Kublai Khan was the Great Khan of the Mongols as well as the founder of the Yuan Dynasty in China. Kublai Khan was in control when the Polo brothers had the great Khan's ear for trade with Europe and the hope of gaining entry into the silk products produced in the region. Kublai had an open mind to religion and wanted to know more about the Christian faith, but much fear had erupted in Europe. Pope Alexander IV announced to Christian Europe in a 1260 Papal Bull that they faced "wars of universal destruction wherewith the scourge of Heaven's wrath in the hands of the inhuman Tartars [the Mongols], erupting as it were from the secret confines of Hell, oppresses and crushes the earth." For men such as the Polos, however, the now stable and peaceful Mongol Empire was a source of wealth, rather than of hellfire.

On their first visit to Kublai Khan's court, the Khan had asked the Polo brothers to bring him oil from the Holy Sepulchre in Jerusalem, which Armenian Orthodox priests sold in that city, so the Polos went to the Holy City to buy the consecrated oil. Instead of returning to the Khan's empire, they held the oils for their next return to Mongolia. They crossed the desert sands in Persia and travelled extensively trading with all races as they made their way back to Venice arriving there on the death of Pope Alexander 1V.

It was fortuitous that a matter of weeks saw the election in 1271, of Pope Gregory X who received the letter from Kublai Khan, remitted by Niccolò and Maffeo Polo. Kublai Khan had asked for the dispatch to his empire of a hundred missionaries and the letter included his request for some oil from the lamp of Jerusalem, and that he wished to learn all he could of the Christian faith.

So it was with the blessing of the newly appointed Pope, that the Polo Brothers with a brief stay in Venice to organise business dealings, left Rustichello in charge of the local business once again, this time with agreements to his terms of trade as he had requested. He specified that he could buy one-third of the produce he negotiated in his name to sell in England as he had wanted to. And so it was that the Polo brothers, merchants of great renown, set sail for Asia with the missionaries on board ship and a barrel of holy oils bound for the Mongolian empire to bring gifts to the Khan of Khans and present him with the Holy oils. Not one hundred missionaries went with them to teach Christianity but only two were appointed by the Pope.

Niccolò also left Rustichello in charge of his son Marco to teach him the skills of being a merchant of Venice in the imports and exports of produce and money flow negotiation skills. However, this was not to be and whilst the Father had refused point blank for his son to travel with him; the determined Marco stowed away on board the ship and was not discovered until days into the voyage and too far away from the port of Venice to turn back. Niccolò was furious with his son and rebuked him, refusing to speak to him for days of that voyage. Marco believed that his father cared more for business dealings than his flesh and blood, and to a great degree, this would prove to be true as the Polos worked in the kingdoms of Mongolia.

The two Polos, this time accompanied by the 17-year-old Marco Polo returned to Mongolia, accompanied by two Dominican friars. The journey took two years to reach Kanbaliq and The Polo's emitted the presents from the Pope to Kublai in 1274. The brother could not honour the request of the great Kahn and in his eyes, they had lied to him, and the two friars did not finish the voyage due to fear, so the Polo merchants arrived empty-handed apart from the Holy oils, which the Khan although having been well-read on the subject He did not appreciate the significance of the holy liquid for baptism, the anointment of the sick and dying and in its use in the ceremonies of vocations to the religious life.

It was the great Khan's wish to punish the Polos for their indiscretions under pain of death, but the emperor took a liking to Marco and asked his advice as to their punishment. Marco had seen the ruthlessness of the Kahn and his guards as well as countless deaths by torture, hanging and fire in his two years on the Silk Road route with his father and uncle. He knew the punishment should be severe enough to gratify the Khan of Khans. So he suggested to the Kublai Khan that they each be tortured with a white-hot iron to their chest branding them as Mendax, which is Latin for liar. The Kahn agreed provided that Marco administered the punishment. Marco without hesitation had his father and uncle kneel before him as he branded their chest with the mark of truth. Niccolo knew that this was necessary for their survival and for their mission of trade in the kingdom to prove successful. Niccolo understood that it was necessary to forgive his son but his uncle never did. In addition to gaining favour, Nicollo offered his son Marco to the Mongol Lord as a servant.

The Polos spent the next 17 years in China. Kublai Khan took a liking to Marco, who was an engaging storyteller. He was sent on many diplomatic missions throughout his empire. Marco carried out diplomatic assignments but also entertained the Khan with interesting stories and observations about the lands he travelled. According to Marco's later travel account as told in 'The Travels of Marco Polo' by Rustichello da Pisa, the Polos asked several times for permission to return to Europe but the great Khan appreciated the visitors so much that he would not agree to their departure.

Marco from time to time, like his father and uncle, fell out of favour with the Khan. Marco's blunder was mistakenly advising the Khan on a new strategy to win a battle which failed due to an incorrect calculation by the young man. So whilst held in prison once more, he devised a plan to use a catapult to send huge boulders of rock to break down the enemy fortress. He used the same principles employed by Alexander the Great and had the idea presented to the Khan. Kublai was duly impressed and put his young charge to the task of building several catapults which proved a success as Marco had predicted.

When he first met Kublai Khan, the founder of the Yuan Dynasty, Marco Polo was just 20 years old. By this time he had become an enthusiastic admirer of the Mongol people, quite at odds with the opinion in most of 13th century Europe. His "Travels" notes that "They are those people who most in the world bear work and great hardship and are content with little food, and who are for this reason suited best to conquer cities, lands, and kingdoms." The Polos had arrived in Kublai Khan's summer capital, called Shangdu or "Xanadu." Marco was overcome by the beauty of the place: "The halls and rooms.. are all gilded and wonderfully painted within with pictures and images of beasts and birds and trees and flowers. It is fortified like a castle in which are fountains and rivers of running water and very beautiful lawns and groves."

Little did the Polos know that they would be forced to remain in Yuan China for seventeen years. They could not leave without Kublai Khan's permission, and he enjoyed conversing with his "pet" Venetians. Marco, in particular, became a favourite of the Khan's and incurred a lot of jealousy from the Mongol courtiers. Kublai Khan was extremely curious about Catholicism, and the Polos believed at times that he might convert. The Khan's mother had been a Nestorian Christian, so it was not so great a leap as it might have appeared. However, conversion to a Western faith might have alienated many of the emperor's subjects, so he toyed with the idea but never committed to it. Marco Polo's descriptions of the wealth and splendour of the Yuan court, and the size and organization of Chinese cities, struck his European audience as impossible to believe. He loved the southern Chinese city of Hangzhou, which at that time had a population of about 1.5 million people.

By the time Kublai Khan reached the age of 75 in 1291, the Polos probably had just about given up hope that he would ever allow them to return home to Europe. He also seemed determined to live forever. Marco, his father, and his uncle finally got permission to leave the Great Khan's court that year, so that they could serve as escorts of a 17-year-old Mongol princess who was being sent to Persia as a bride.

The travels of Marco Polo may not have ever been told if fate had not taken a hand in the next stage of his life of travel. Marco Polo was a great verbal storyteller of his time and his adventures. He worked on a manuscript entitled "The Travels of Marco Polo" which retold to Rustichello da Pisa, his good friend and elder former business guide, how he spent the years in the courts and diplomatic service in war and peace in the kingdom of the great Kublai Khan, emperor and Khan of Khans. It was some years after his return to Venice when they were both imprisoned by the Genoans on the northwest coast of Italy after joining the war against the Italian mainland that that story unfolded. It is not unfair to say that Marco Polo's story of his adventures as an exporter, merchant, diplomat for the Emperor of the Mongol empire, Kublai Khan of Khans, soldier of fortune, leader and engineer of great war machine skills could easily be granted the title 'Master of the Arts,' but the book of his travels, be they of his imagination to a great degree or of fact can be disputed, just as easily as the fiction of the story of Rustichello da Pisa that I tell here in my opinion of the Master of the Arts.

Polo's adventures are recounted in Rustichello's biographer's writings, *The Travels*, where he describes the peoples, places, and customs of the East, including the fabulous court of the Khan. The work caused a sensation and was one of the principal factors in creating a lasting image in European minds that China was a fabulous land of wealth and exotica, almost too fantastic to be believed. Even if doubts remain as to just where he travelled to and what he saw with his own eyes, Marco Polo continues to enjoy a reputation as the world's greatest-ever explorer and provides invaluable insights into Mongol rule and Asia in general in the late 13th century.

CHAPTER 9.

HOMEWARD BOUND.

The Polos took the sea route back, first boarding a ship to Sumatra, now in Indonesia, where they were marooned by changing monsoons for 5 months. Once the winds shifted, they went on to Ceylon (Sri Lanka), and then to India, where Marco was fascinated by Hindu cow-worship and mystical yogis, along with Jainism and its prohibition on harming even a single insect. From there, they voyaged on to the Arabian Peninsula, arriving back at Hormuz, where they delivered the princess to her waiting bridegroom. It took two years for them to make the trip from China back to Venice; thus, Marco Polo likely was just about to turn 40 when he returned to his home city, a world-weary but wiser man now.

As imperial emissaries and savvy traders, the Polos returned to Venice in 1295 laden with exquisite goods. However, Venice was embroiled in a feud with Genoa over control of the very trade routes that had enriched the Polos. Thus it was that Marco found himself in command of a Venetian war galley, and then a prisoner of the Genoese.

Marco's loyalties to his home city of Venice remained strong, and the adventurer fought in the war against Venice's long-time rival Genoa, serving as a sea captain. Marco was wounded and captured by the Genoese in 1296 or 1298 CE. He was then imprisoned, but at least this allowed him to put down in writing his epic adventures in Asia. Well, it was not him but a friend and fellow inmate who did the writing, one Rustichello da Pisa, who followed Marco's dictation based on his private notes made in Asia, which are referred to several times in the text itself.

As we have heard and all accounts according to Marco Polo's notes 'In 1271 CE, then aged just 17, Marco accompanied his father and uncle, Niccoló and Maffeo, on what was the elder men's second journey to East Asia, visiting the court of the Mongol leader Kublai Khan in China.'Polo would go on to venture far beyond the confines of his native Europe, traversing vast and mysterious lands whose existence was but a whisper in the Western world.

His extraordinary journey – from the Byzantine grandeur of Constantinople to the distant court of the Mongol emperor, Kublai Khan, and beyond – would forever transform the European understanding of the world.

Polo's writings, collected in the book known as "The Travels of Marco Polo" or "Il Milione", presented the East in unprecedented detail. It was not just a chronicle of geographical features or diplomatic affairs; it was an all-encompassing exploration of the region's cultures, languages, traditions, and commerce. His vivid accounts of the far-reaching Silk Road and life under the Mongol Empire provided a window into a world that was otherwise inaccessible to his contemporaries.

1269, when Marco was around fifteen years old, his father and uncle returned from the East with wondrous tales of distant lands and a mission from Kublai Khan himself. Intrigued by their stories, young Marco found himself standing at the precipice of a vast unknown world, one he would soon come to know in great detail. The elder Polos' voyage was commissioned by Kublai Khan, the fifth Khagan of the Mongol Empire, who had requested they return with scholars and priests to teach Christianity and Western customs to his court.

Setting sail from Venice, they journeyed through the Mediterranean Sea and reached the rugged lands of the Middle East, following the established routes of the Silk Road. They travelled through Armenia, Persia and Afghanistan, across the Pamir Mountains and the formidable Taklamakan Desert, sometimes called "The Desert of Death." Throughout this journey, young Marco Polo was introduced to a plethora of cultures and customs vastly different from his own. He encountered various religious practices, a myriad of languages, and a diverse range of goods, enriching his understanding of the world with every step. There, they crossed paths with tribes and communities living under Mongol rule, witnessing first-hand the extent and influence of the empire. Marco documented the customs, traditions, and lifestyles of these people, marking the beginnings of his rich ethnographic observations that would later make his travel accounts invaluable.

After his release from prison in 1299, Marco Polo returned to Venice and continued his work as a merchant. He never went travelling again, however, he hired others to make expeditions instead of taking on that task himself.

Marco Polo also married the daughter of another successful trading family and had three daughters.

Kublai had created the largest empire the world had ever seen, with Mongol rule extending from the Caspian Sea to the Korean peninsula. Kublai's permanent capital was Cambaluc on the site of modern Beijing and his court was famous for its splendour. The Khan was known as a keen supporter of literature, he favoured Buddhism as his belief but he permitted all religions to be practised, and he embraced Chinese culture, unlike his predecessors. In short, the Khan was an ideal host to welcome such a traveller as Marco Polo.

The young Venetian would be suitably admiring in his description of the Khan in his travel notes: "Kublai, who is styled grand khan, or lord, is of middle stature, that is, neither tall nor short; his limbs are well formed, and in his whole figure, there is a just proportion. His complexion is fair and occasionally suffused with red, like the bright tint of the rose, which adds much grace to his countenance. His eyes are black and handsome, his nose is well-shaped and prominent."The admiration must have been mutual as Marco was appointed a permanent and roving envoy of the Khan, a move in keeping with the Mongol ruler's policy of not using Chinese officials when possible. It seems that, just as Marco would wow Europe with his tales of the East later in life, so, too, he was destined to travel to the further parts of the Mongol Empire and then return to the Khan and inform him of the people and customs he had encountered. He learnt local languages, took extensive notes in his role as the Khan's envoy, and was perhaps even made deputy governor of Yang Chow, a post he held for three years (although some scholars maintain he resided there in some other capacity).

Marco proved to be a man of many talents, at least that is what he claimed in his own words, for he not only engineered great weapons for battle but led troops into battle on the Khans' behalf, becoming for a time his chief guide and adviser in the court of the Khan, was sent far and wide on diplomatic service and was the Khan of Khans trusted servant, an honour never before given to a foreigner. Marco, if his many tales of his travels and talents in the service of the Mongol emperor are true, could well be called the 'Master of Arts' but for this story, this author of imaginary tales would prefer to continue to give that ethical honour to Rustichello da Pisa, Philosopher, Merchant of Venice, writer of the 'Tales of King Arthur and his Knights' and " The Travels of Marco Polo'

Somehow Marco's later romantic tales of adventure resulted in the successful writing of Rustichello da Pisa's' The Travels of Marco Polo" which was
widely read at the time. as was a romantic tale based loosely on Xanadu,
the kingdom of Philip 111 of France, his adventures in excruciating the
sword of Roland's Durandal from a rock. The mythical tale of Camelot,
King Arthur and his Knights. of the Round Table, of Lancelot and Guine-
vere's romance, and the plot of Mordred the rebellious nephew of King
Arthur who captured the Queen and raised a rebellion against the kingdom.
not to mention the similarities and differences between Excalibur, King
Arthur's magic sword to the magic sword of Roland as both were extracted
from a rock by the hero of the day. And of course, there is always a wizard
somewhere in any good romantic fairytale.

Encompassing a twenty-four-year period from 1271, Polo's account to Rustichello da Pisa whilst they shared a prison cell, details his travels in the
service of the empire, from Beijing to northern India and ends with the re-
markable story of Polo's return voyage from the Chinese port of Amoy to
the Persian Gulf. Before his death, Polo admitted that he made up most of
the tales he told Europeans. Most believed the book was written not by him
but but Kublai Khan himself. The fact was he co-wrote the book or at least
was the teller of his tales to the author Rustichello who was for a time considered a criminal by some, perhaps because of his time in prison.

Marco Polo's travel route was significant because it helped to open the flow
of goods and ideas from east to west. Europe was in a period called the
Middle Ages, however, because the Mongolian Empire had control of China, inventions such as the compass and gunpowder would eventually make
their way to Western Europe.

During his 17 years in China, Marco Polo observed the use of paper money,
the postal system, coal, eyeglasses, and impressive architecture such as the
Mongolian palaces, in particular in Xanadu."The Travels of Marco Polo"
described these innovations in the book after he returned to Europe. Polo's
accounts of his experiences in China and other parts of Asia and his details
of being in service to The Khan of Khans provided valuable insights into
the outside world. Lastly, Polo's willingness to adapt to the Mongol way of
life and his loyalty to Kublai Khan further extended his stay in Asia as a
diplomat in service to the ruler.

Polo was soon freed after the war between Venice and the Genoese and he returned to Venice. The remainder of his life can be reconstructed, in part, through the testimony of legal documents. He seems to have led a quiet existence, managing a not-too-conspicuous fortune. In January of 1324, Marco Polo died at the age of 69. In his will, he freed a "Tartar slave" who had served him since his return from China. Although the man had died, his story lived on, inspiring the imaginations and adventures of other Europeans. Christopher Columbus, for example, had a copy of Marco Polo's "Travels," which he notated heavily in the margins. Whether or not they believed his stories, the people of Europe certainly loved to hear about the fabulous Kublai, the Khan of Khans and his wondrous courts at Xanadu, his summer capital, an idealised place with idyllic magnificence and beauty.

Some historians argue that Marco Polo went by the nickname, 11 Milioni meaning 'million,' but others believe that this was a title applied later by people who thought that his book contained a 'million lies' On his deathbed, Marco Polo was asked by a priest to admit what the world already knew: that he had stretched the truth about his travels. The old voyager is said to have shot back, " I have not told even half of what I saw." He died, but he did not give up the spirit.

Rustichello was there in spirit only at the black Mass service for the funeral of Marco Polo. He had predeceased Marco Polo by some 24 years. The Chiesa di Santa Maria Assunta detta I Gesuiti Church pews were packed with local merchants, political leaders, friends and family. If he had been present the kindly Master of the Arts would no doubt have fought back tears as he listened to the officiating priest tell of the life of a much loved but sometimes criticised adventurer. He knew Marco best and the longest of any of them all. Rustichello I imagine would have written more of his association with Marco before his father and uncles' return to Venice from their first voyage and long travelling venture in the Far East. He would possibly have recalled the intelligence of the young boy, and his willingness to work hard and learn what he could of the merchant business. He had been given the additional duty of guiding and protecting the young sixteen-year-old as the Polo brothers headed to sea on the next voyage to Asia.

Old parchments confirm The Master of the Arts had carried on the business for the Polo brothers' merchant of Venice for the supply and export of produce on their behalf throughout Europe and Britain for the next seventeen years without the assistance of Marco. So on their return from Asia after a year on the open sea Marco, with his father and uncle, finally reached the city of Venice in 1295. When they arrived they found their freight transport vessels in dry dock for Venice was at war with the Italian city of Genoa at the time. The seaport on the northwest coast of Italy had blocked all trade through the ports of Italy except their own. A letter written by Rustichello to Niccolò, and his uncle Maffeo explained that he had no option but to go to war to fight the infidels who were ruining the trade of merchants and in particular their business.

Rustichello advised in the letter that he had taken his vessels with a small number of Templar Knights and merchants who were willing to join the fight. and had headed for the battle by the sea weeks before the Polo returned. So Marco Polo, never one to back down in a fight, entered the war as a ship's captain on one of his father's Caravelle ships but was soon captured and imprisoned by the Genoese seafaring natives of their busy seaport.

It was much later, as Rustichello recalled, he realised that the forces of the seafaring Genoese were far too strong for his volunteer inexperienced sailors and Template Knights then decided to anchor the ship away towards the south of the Genoese port city and continue the journey on foot. He recalls how he and his band of fighters went to battle under his charge and overpowered a great number of the enemy before the reinforcements of the Genoese far outnumbered their own. He in his imagination as an old man had considered that had he had the singing sword of magic quality of Rolands's Durendal, the outcome of the battles would have more than likely been won in his favour.

Rustichello later recalled in notes that he had written to Niccolò Polo
I searched everywhere throughout the streets of Venice, the shops, bars and churches, Finally at the Port of Venice where your ship had departed the dock I found the answer to your missing son Marco Polo. A sailor in a bar, whilst packing the cargo for your voyage told me he had sighted the boy hanging about the docks and later he saw him climb aboard the ship unnoticed by the crew, or you or your brother. He said he lost sight of him after that and presumed he had got off the boat before it sailed. It was obvious to me that Marco had stowed away and hid in the cargo hull until later discovered. This letter was found some seventeen years later when the Polos had returned to their business dealings during the war with Genoa.

So it was that Marco Polo while in prison met up with his one-time mentor known thereafter as the Master of Arts and well-known writer of romantic tales, one Rustichello da Pisa. So it was during their two-year imprisonment in the war with Genoa that Marco Polo shared his adventures throughout the unknown world which resulted in the author and co-writer producing a documented story " The Travels of Marco Polo "

Earlier, Rustichello had written a work in French known as the Roman de Roi Artus (Romance of King Arthur) or simply the Compilation, derived from a book in the possession of Edward I of England, who passed through Italy on his way to fight in the Eighth Crusade in 1270-1274. The Compilation contains an interpolation of the expedition against Troy, which was told in Greek mythology. A fable unfolded of a mythical hero who joined the trust of Greece in the story. The fight in the now-fragmentary prose account of Arthur's Saracen knight Palamedes and the history of the Round Table. It was later divided into two sections, named after their principal protagonists, Meliadus (Tristan's father) and Guiron le Courtois; these remained popular for hundreds of years and influenced works written in French as well as in Spanish, Italian, and even Greek.

The book "The Travels of Marco Polo" was an instant success—"In a few months it spread throughout Italy," wrote Giovanni Battista Ramusic, the 16th-century Italian geographer—*Il milione* was conceived as a vast cosmography based on firsthand experience. The book was not intended to be a collection of personal recollections, which leaves Polo's personality somewhat elusive, but *Divisament dou monde* ("Description of the World"), as it was originally titled, was to be the book to end all books on Asia. Nonetheless, details concerning travel, distances covered, and seasons are rarely stated; the panorama is observed from an impersonal distance with a powerful wide-angle lens. In *Il milione* Polo often branches off into descriptions of places probably visited not by himself but by his relatives or people he knew. Typical digressions are those in Mesopotamia, the assassins and their castles, in Samarkand, Siberia, Japan and Madagascar. *Il milione* is better understood not as a biography but as part of the venally alar vernacular, of which the Middle Ages offer many examples.

The work is marked by uncertainty and controversy, however. The origin of the popular title, *Il milione*, for example, is not quite clear. Although it most likely comes from Polo's nickname, *Il Milione*, from his tendency to describe the millions of things he saw in the Mongol empire, it may have been related to the idea of a "tall story," or from a nickname running in the family, possibly traceable to a corruption of Aemilione ("Big Emil"). The history of the text itself is characterized by similar uncertainty. There is no authentic original manuscript, and even if there were, it would likely not represent what Polo dictated since Rustichello asserted his personality and familiar phraseology, especially in the standardized description of battles. Polo also seems to have made amendments himself on various copies of the work during the last 20 years or so of his life. Some editors—for instance, the friar Pipino, who made a good Latin translation of the original—found many of Polo's descriptions or interpretations impious or dangerously near to heresy and therefore heavily removed text that he considered bold or offensive.

Furthermore, since all this happened long before the invention of printing professional scribes or amateurs made dozens of copies of the book, as well as free translations and adaptations—often adding to or subtracting from the text with little or no respect for authenticity. Many unfamiliar names rarely passed unchanged from one copy to another. Consequently, there are some 140 different manuscript versions of the text in three manuscript groups, in a dozen different languages and dialects—an immensely complex and controversial body of material representing one of the most unyielding philological problems inherited from the Middle Ages.

At any rate, the tales were enough to allow Rustichello to whittle away his dotage in the realm of his fertile imagination which was to bring him to great acclaim as a writer, philosopher and in his old age as a retiree, be that a short-lived one for he died in 1300 at age 50. He had been respected once as a Merchant of Venice and bore the title Master of the Arts. And although this tale is more fiction than fact, as may be 'The Travels of Marco Polo,' it goes without saying that in life, more so today than yesteryear, one must be a man of many talents, a master of many arts to make it in an even faster-changing world.

This story Master of the Arts is likewise a fragmented account that came to me as an idea based on the difficulty in modern life to focus on a single career objective as was the case in my formative years, education and working life. It was not an issue back then to leave a job and change direction as work was plentiful and jobs secure throughout the decades from the 1960s to the early 2000s. was almost guaranteed. I have had the fortune of being educated in a variety of career opportunities and it was my habit of changing career direction multiple times over my working life even though that was out of character for most of my generation. So with an idea of the need for multiple skills today in mind, it was not much of a leap of faith to view it from the heights of a retiree seat now in leisure and looking back at the past seeing how rapidly work life is changing. And now in the age of Artificial Intelligence, one has to become even more adaptive. So it is that as this story unfolded I make no excuse for dabbling in the history books and remembering tales of my youth to help in the telling.

.

"Consult not your fears but your hopes and your dreams. Think not about your frustrations, but about your unfulfilled potential. Concern yourself not with what you tried and failed in, but with what it is still possible for you to do."

—Pope John XX111

CHAPTER 10.

EPILOGUE

It must be said that I was a lover of Shakespeare in my youth and formal years in high school. So the story of the Merchant of Venice, and those of King Arthur and his knights as written by Geoffrey of Monmouth, whose 12th-century account of Arthur's life was Europe's most popular text after the Bible, greatly influenced me. Of course, the comic classics of my boyhood also helped me in my herein fictional tale. Later the 1968 film Camelot gave the visual impact to feed my imagination even further.

Then in walking the Camino de Santiago in 2013, 2015 and 2017 I was well-groomed to General Charlemagne's battles with the Moors and the song of Roland and his magic sword Durendal, as I was to King Arthur's magical Excalibur. It should not be forgotten that Rustichello de Pisa wrote in the latter part of the thirteenth century, translated or compiled what perhaps is the earliest Arthurian romances written by an Italian. He recounts in prose the chivalric exploits of Tristan, the mighty feats of Tristan's father Meliadus, together with knights such as Lancelot and Gurion le Courtois.

As sources from the Arthurian legends Rustichello, translating from Latin into French, claimed that he used the words of Luces de Gast, and those of Roberta and Helie de Boron to add to his fictions writings. To the romance of prose, Rustichello also added lengthy fragments of the prose of Tristan, and other accounts including stories of the death of King Mark. The encyclopaedic collection of this and other information is frequently mentioned in old inventories and catalogues.

So it is with the story of Roland The *Song of Roland* is one of the most studied works in French literature. Oxford, Bodleian Library preserves the oldest extant secular narrative in a modern European language, in this case Anglo-Norman French. The name *Song of Roland* was assigned to the Oxford text in the early 19th century. This earliest version of the poem is generally accepted as the finest and most important example not only of the Roland story but of a *chanson de geste*, a major genre of 12th- and 13th-century French literature. Indeed, the Oxford *Roland* is one of the great texts of the European Middle Ages, a masterpiece of structure, style, narrative, and poetic expression. Originally studied largely for its historical interest as a beacon of the cultural and political origins of a French national spirit, in the early 20th century the poem began a lengthy existence as a scholarly battleground between "traditionalists," who saw the poem as a product of centuries of anonymous oral composition, and "originalists," who judged the Oxford text to be the composition of a single brilliant poet.

So you can glean that I have written this fictional account of the Master of Arts from a variety of historical sources to fire up the imagination on the life of both Rustichello da Pisa and Marco Polo, as well as ideas from modern writings. I make no apology for dipping into the well of information available on the subject matter of my account of the facts and fictional characters in this novel. I trust that you the reader gain some measure of enjoyment in the reading of what I entrust to you as a ''good yarn,' but equally as a motivator to you if you need a new direction in life or current employment, to heed the message herein of the Master of Arts.

Much of the themes of this book centre around the importance of myth, though it is mentioned sparingly in the body of the story except to shed light on the power of the sword to honour historically, to cement the importance of its symbolism into perpetuity. The sword symbolised power and protection. authority, strength and courage; metaphysically, it represents discrimination and the penetrating power of the intellect. The sword is phallic, with the sheath being shaped artificially like a place for copulation and rebirth It is a symbol of knighthood and chivalry.

In the Camino de Santiago, the story of the song of Roland and that of King Arthur and his knights, Shakespeare's Merchant of Venice subconsciously influences the writer's use of the sword almost as a subplot to its importance in myth, folklore and legend.

Life brings with it many highs and lows as in the aforementioned stories. It seems to me that to make progress in life we need to suffer much to change, surrender to get well in body, mind and spirit and to find acceptance we must practice many things to succeed in life. None of it comes without a symbolic influence, it comes with serenity and reason and it is in these examples many a sword comes into the frame.

We have many mythical accounts throughout history where swords are used symbolically in ceremonies, and for good or for evil purposes. It is worthy of consideration if it is justified in this enlightened age to put away the sword forever. It is often stated that the pen is mightier than the sword and as one who writes I am very mindful of that. It is so easy to fool oneself into believing the myth in every tale, being seduced into a lie by the words on a page. We are moving now ever so quickly into the world of artificial Intelligence allowing the computer 'thoughts' to do our thinking for us.

If we are to make progress for the better, then it is fine to use myth, legend and folklore to make a point or entertain, but not at the risk of being deceived by a lie, for when we wield a sword we are in danger of thus cutting ourselves. In all written work be it economic, political, religious, environmental or any issue for the knowledge and understanding of humanity, let the truth always prevail. But with this new wave of artificial intelligence taking over where journalism left off, we can easily be deceived by myth. legend and folklore at the expense of the truth. So dear reader. pay heed to what you discern and consider what you will sacrifice for truth. " What will you sacrifice for truth?"

The moving finger writes and having writ moves on....

About the Author.

Doug McPhillips, poet, singer, songwriter, and author, commenced his journey of discovery over a decade ago after life-changing experiences.

The many tracks he has traversed through the Northern Hemisphere and down under in Australia and New Zealand have resulted in the facts and fiction of this novel.

Doug has recorded and sung songs inter-relateded to his many works with majestic melodies in a true Australian style

Doug has written several novels, two books of poems, a travel guide and three albums of his songs all inspired by his adventurers.

Doug is an adventurer who divides his time between family and friends, his creative pursuits, and those who benefit most from his efforts and experience.

Check out the synopsis of stories of this author on the web-
caminoway.com.au and at all online bookstores and libraries

The ISBNs for each of the books are on the site for both
paperbacks and ebooks.

Worldwide Publisher,

IngramSpark
1 La Verge TN37086
Nashville, Tennessee.

Printed in Australia
Lightning Source
76 Discovery Road South
Scoresby, Victoria 3179